WHAT THE ORANGUTAN TOLD ALICE

WHAT THE ORANGUTAN TOLD ALICE

by Dale Smith

Photographs by Dale Smith & Anne E. Russon

DEER
CREEK
PUBLISHING
NEVADA CITY, CALIFORNIA

Published by
Deer Creek Publishing
P.O. Box 2594
Nevada City, CA 95959

Telephone: (530) 478-1758; FAX: (530) 478-1759;
email: deercrk@pacbell.net; web site: www.deercreekpublishing.com

This book is a work of environmental fiction. Though some names, characters, places and
incidents may be recognizable, what the characters say and where they say it are products
of the author's imagination. Any resemblance to actual events or locales or persons, living or dead, is coincidental.

ISBN: 0-9651452-8-X
Library of Congress Catalog Card Number (LCCN): 2001 130533

Smith, Dale, 1945
  What the Orangutan Told Alice: a rain forest adventure :
  a novel / by Dale Smith -- 1st ed.
  p. cm
SUMMARY: In Indonesian Borneo, Alice discovers the
plight of the orangutans who are losing their
habitat--and being poached by illegal hunters for the
pet trade.
  Audience: Grades 6-12
  Audience: Ages 11-17
  ISBN 0-9651452-8-X

  1. Orangutan--Juvenile fiction. 2 Poaching--Juvenile fiction. 3. Wild animal trade--
Juvenile fiction. 4. Endangered species--Juvenile fiction. 5. Kalimantan Selatan
(Indonesia)--Juvenile fiction. 6. Orangutan--Fiction. 9. Endangered species--Fiction. 10.
Kalimantan Selantan (Indonesia)--Fiction. I.
Title.

PZ7.S64467Wha 2001   [Fic]
                        QBI01-700381

Book design by Dale Smith
Manufactured in the United States of America

10 9 8 7 6 5 4 3 2 1

Contents

For Anne,
and Panjul's memory.

The worst thing that can happen—will happen—is not energy
depletion, economic collapse, limited nuclear war, or conquest by
a totalitarian government. As terrible as these catastrophes would be
for us, they can be repaired within a few generations. The process
ongoing in the 1980s that will take millions of years to correct is the
loss of genetic and species diversity by destruction of natural habitats.
This is the folly our descendants are least likely to forgive us.

Edward O. Wilson
Harvard University

In the end we will conserve only what we love.
We will love only what we understand.
We will understand only what we have been taught.

Baba Dioum

Acknowledgements

Writing this book would have been impossible without *access*—access to the Wanariset Orangutan Reintroduction Center on the island of Borneo, access to the Sungai Wain and Mertaus release forests, and access to the people who know the truth about orangutans and their plight.

Thanks to Christine Luckett of the Balikpapan Orangutan Society, who e-mailed me early on that if I wanted to know what was really happening with orangutans in Borneo, I should come see for myself.

I am indebted to Dr. Anne E. Russon for sharing her knowledge, insights, stories and photographs with me. I am also grateful to Willie Smits, the founder of the Wanariset Orangutan Reintroduction Center, for his invaluable assistance and incredible stories, and for permitting me to visit so many special places.

Thanks to Connie Breeze for editing the manuscript.

Thanks also to Pak Adi Susilo, Aschta Nita Boestani, Jeane Mandala, Rondang of Wanariset and Martinus de Kam of Tropenbos, for allowing me access to the orangutan refugees at Wanariset.

Behind the scenes are the veterinarians and forest technicians who toil tirelessly under difficult and primitive conditions at both Wanariset and in the release forests. To Bedi, Muhan, Sam Edry, Augustino, Rachman, Haris, Ical, Suciyonto, Dolan, Muloko, Dr. Amir, Dr. Jumintarto, Siti, Trisno, Iyan, Fandi and the legions of others, thank you for your time.

During my visits to Wanariset I met several students who were studying orangutans. Many valuable insights into the lives and behavior of orangutans were gleaned over dinners at "Ani's Café." For their conversational contributions I would like to acknowledge and thank Andy Antilla of the Woodland Zoo in Seattle, Julia Le Neve Foster and Kirrily de Polnay of Oxford Universtiy, French graduate students Sophie Mounier and Emmanuelle (Miss Nest) Grundman and butterfly expert Danny Cleary.

I would also like to thank BOS-USA members Michael & Wayne Sowards, Shirley Randolph, Sarita Siegel, Cheryl Knott and Christine Mallar for their support and help in writing this book. And thanks to Tim Laman for his tips on photographing orangutans in the rain forest.

Thanks, too, to Dr. Shirley McGreal of the International Primate Protection League for suggesting, back in 1996, that I write this book.

Thanks also to Jay-Dee Ake, JudyAnne Andress, LeeAnn Brook, Christy Butterfield, Suzanna Camejo, Brion Dunbar, David Fritz, Kathy Gillivand, Susan Glover, Jan Holder, Jack Izzo, S.J., Larry and Lisa Keenan, Laurel and Tom Lippert, Steve Lowe, Michael McClure, Linda Millercox, John Packer and Bonnie St. James for their input and support along the way.

Lastly, thanks to my daughter Alice and our friend Shane for their inspirational roles in this story.

Dale Smith
Nevada City, California

Where in the world is Indonesia?

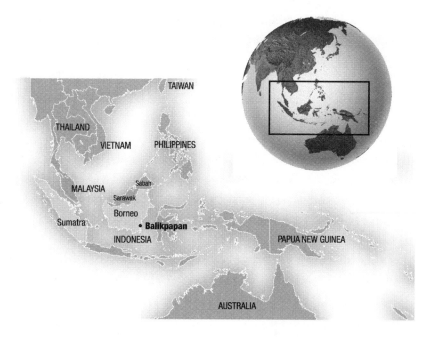

Being There

When Alice Smith tucked her long legs beneath her body, the high-backed rattan chair in which she sat responded with a mournful creak. In her fourteen years she could not remember being as uncomfortable as she was at that moment, as she sat in the dark, mahogany paneled living room of the guesthouse her father had rented for their stay in Indonesian Borneo. The city of Balikpapan, just south of the equator on the southeastern coast of the earth's third largest island, was the hottest, most humid place she had ever been. It was more sweltering than Las Vegas in August and muggier than Panama, where the atmosphere had been so thick with moisture she'd expected to see fish swimming through the air.

Directly above Alice's creaky chair, an overhead fan wobbled noisily at the end of its frayed cord. The wooden blades, their leading edges caked with fuzzy dust, did not generate enough breeze to blow a mosquito off course.

Alice pulled a bandanna from her pocket and mopped the beads of sweat from her brow. She yawned, mostly out of boredom but partly from jet lag, and reached for the bottle of water on the coffee table. "Drink lots of water, and wait here until I get back. And don't leave the house." Those were the words her

Here's where it all started, the guesthouse my dad and I
stayed in near Balikpapan in Indonesian Borneo. A.S.

father had said before he left for his breakfast meeting. As quickly as Alice guzzled the lukewarm water, it seemed to ooze from her every pore as if she were some kind of human sieve. Perspiration beaded her upper lip, and sweat trickled from her scalp and under her arms and flowed down the side of her ribcage. It coursed down her slender neck like a miniature flash flood, between her shoulder blades and down the middle of her chest. So efficiently did her body process her intake of water that she hadn't felt the urge to urinate since yesterday, when she and her father had arrived in the Indonesian province of East Kalimantan. She sighed and shook her head, unable to believe she was actually in Borneo.

She thought back to the cool evening just a month ago, when her father had taken her out for sushi and told her that they would be traveling to Borneo that summer.

"Borneo?" Alice had said as she struggled to control her chopsticks. "Like where is Borneo, anyway?"

"In the southern hemisphere, just below the equator," her father said patiently, "is a huge ocean and in that vast body of water is an archipelago and one of the seventeen thousand islands in that chain is called Borneo, and that's where we're headed."

"Oh, I know where it is," said Alice, remembering a geography lesson. "But why? Why do we have to go there?"

"Because that's where the orangutans live," said her dad, who wanted to learn all he could about Asia's mysterious red ape for a book he hoped to write. "On the growing list of the earth's endangered species, the orangutan is right near the top."

"Can't you just go to the library and like, read about them?" said Alice as a lump of rice tumbled from her chopsticks into the small bowl of soy sauce on her plate.

"No," said her father. "Just reading about them wouldn't be the same as actually seeing them. If you're going to learn about orangutans, you've got to go into the forest where the orangutans live and hang out with them. And the only places in the world they live are two islands, Borneo and Sumatra."

"Oh," said Alice. "It's kind of too bad they don't live in Hawaii."

"What are you saying—you don't want to go to Borneo?"

"Uh, not really. I'd rather spend the summer with my friends."

"Don't be such a homebo, Alice," said her father, using the word Alice had invented some years ago to describe her preference to stay home. "It'll be fun, just you and me, father and daughter, off on a great adventure. Tell me, how many of your friends do you think get the chance to go to Borneo?"

"None, zip, zero, nada," said Alice. "Their parents take them to Disneyland for vacation."

"I've taken you to Disneyland," said her father, a little defensively.

"What, once, when I was like two?"

"Cut me some slack, Al. Studying orangutans in their natural habitat is going to be a lot of fun. But it's going to be hard work, too, and I need your help. You don't want me lugging my heavy camera gear around by myself, do you?"

Alice rolled her eyes. "Hire someone," she said.

"Hey, where's your sense of adventure?"

"Dad, you're weird. Can't we just go someplace, you know, normal?"

"Normal? And what'd be the point of that? Just imagine what it'll be like, Alice. Borneo's one of the most interesting places in the world. There are snakes there that fly, and fish that climb trees. Don't you want to see some of those amazing animals?"

"Not really," said Alice with a sigh, folding her arms across her chest in an attitude of prepubescent resistance.

"When did you turn into a teenager on me?" said Alice's dad. "That's what I'd like to know."

"I've been a teenager for a couple of years, Dad," said Alice.

Borneo had not exactly been an easy place to get to, which explained why the island was not infested with tourists and resort hotels. The flight from San Francisco had taken 23 hours. First they'd flown to Hong Kong, and then on to the island nation of Singapore. In Singapore they changed to a smaller plane and flew southeast toward Balikpapan.

Alice, slouched into a window seat in the aft section of the half-empty aircraft, had been peering through the scratched window at gargoyle-headed thunderheads when she caught her first glimpse of Borneo far below. She could see nothing but trees, stretching to the horizon like a dark green carpet. There were no roads to be seen, no freeways cutting through the outback. She saw broad rivers the color of chocolate milk, and smaller tributaries that looped and turned back on each other, dividing the forest into puzzle-shaped pieces. Here and there patches of ochre earth came into view, bare yellow clay where trees had once stood, with webs of spidery logging roads crisscrossing the barren soil. The only signs of civilization Alice could see were the tiny tin roofs of small buildings glinting in the sun, laid out in perfectly rectangular grids on patches of land that had been scraped bare. But mostly there were trees, miles and miles of trees. What was all the fuss about, she wondered, all the cries of save the rain forest? From her seat on the plane, it looked as if there were plenty of rain forests in Borneo. But as the plane dropped lower on its approach into Balikpapan, she saw that many of the trees were actually planted in rows. Now, as she heard the landing gear grind down and watched the wing flaps adjust for their landing, she saw rows and rows of green palm fronds swaying in the breeze like feather dusters.

Zzzzzzt. A mosquito whined past Alice's ear and snapped her out of her daydream. To make less of her body available to the mosquitoes, Alice was wearing a thin shirt made of the latest moisture-wicking fabric and lightweight trousers that gathered tightly around her ankles. But her made-for-the-tropics outfit clung to her body like a second skin. She extended her lower lip and blew a flow of cooling breath over her face. The thought occurred to her that if she were going to survive the tropics, she would have to completely rethink how she felt about sweat, hers and everyone else's.

Her father's meeting that morning was with the Director of the Forestry Research Institute. He hoped the Director would grant him permission to visit the restricted forest where ex-captive and orphaned orangutans that had gone through a rehabilitation process were released. In recent years the orangutan had not just climbed to the top of the endangered species list, it now teetered on the edge of extinction. Ten years, her dad said, that's all the time the orangutans have left unless dramatic action is taken to save them. Ten years, thought Alice. Let's see, she'd be twenty-four and her dad, he'd be, well, old.

Though Alice would never admit it, she secretly hoped the Director of the Forestry Research Institute would deny her father's request. And, if she were to be completely truthful, she'd also have to admit that she'd just as soon he'd forget about the orangutans and write a book about some endangered species closer to home. If her father had decided to write a book about desert tortoises, she'd be lounging by the pool of a Las Vegas resort right now, working on her tan. But no, her father had developed an orangutan fixation, and now here she was sweating it out in a dingy little guesthouse that smelled like mildew and where half the time the water didn't flow when she turned the faucet handles.

She couldn't stand the sticky heat a moment longer. She realized it was time for a... what was the Indonesian word for it? Oh yeah, a mandi.

Alice pushed open the bathroom door, flicked on the light and watched in horror as a three-inch cockroach scurried mechanically across the tile floor and dived into the open drain in the corner of the tiny room. "Whoa," she said aloud, "I'm not alone." In one corner of the bathroom, beneath a dripping faucet, stood a waist-high orange plastic tub filled with water. A blue plastic scoop floated on the water's surface. The room's white tiles had faded over the years to a yellow custard color, and the grout that held them in place was streaked with mildew. In the corner next to the tub stood a western-style toilet. The seat on the toilet was disturbingly absent. There was a round hole in the porcelain tank where a flush lever should have been. Stored inside the empty tank, rust-colored from days when it was a fully functioning toilet, was a well-worn toilet bowl brush. Flushing the toilet required pouring water into the toilet bowl.

Alice slipped out of her clothes and hung them, along with her toilet kit and towel, on the corroded metal hook on the back of the door. The floor was slimy beneath her feet and she wished she had thought to wear her sandals. She peered into the orange tub. The water was a little cloudy, but at least she could see the bottom. She dipped the plastic scoop into the water, then poured the water over her head. The cold water was bracing, but it felt wonderful as it cascaded over her body. She poured more water over herself, then took the all-purpose liquid peppermint soap out of her toiletry kit and lathered her hair and body. Then she poured water over her head again and again, and watched the suds carry the sweat and insect repellent down the drain into a netherworld of cockroaches and who-knew-what-else. Alice had to admit that she liked the way the Indonesians bathed. Just as she could not remember being quite so overwhelmed by heat and humidity, she also could not remember feeling as refreshed as she did at that moment after her mandi. She also knew the feeling would not last.

Alice rubbed her head and dried her body vigorously with her towel, then pulled her shoulder-length, honey-blond hair into a ponytail, securing it with a red scrunchy. She peered at her reflection in the cracked mirror on the wall and drew her lips back over her teeth to expose her braces. How much longer was she doomed to wear these things, she wondered? Her orthodontist kept adding time to the length of her sentence, claiming that Alice was not wearing her headgear enough. Well, she supposed her orthodontist had a point. She hadn't been wearing it during the day as she was supposed to. But she couldn't help it. The brightly colored elastic harness that held the headgear in place and the colored bands on her braces were supposed to make her feel better about wearing them, but they didn't. I'll wear it later, she promised herself as she pulled on yet another set of fresh clothes. In the living room she settled again into the rattan chair and picked up an old *Time* magazine from the coffee table. She closed the snaps at her trouser ankles and then folded her legs beneath her, trying to get comfortable again on the chair, which moaned with her every move. Bored, Alice flipped through the magazine back to front but stopped suddenly when she came to a black-and-white photograph of a gorilla.

Reading the story that accompanied the photograph. Alice learned that a four-year-old boy had fallen into the gorilla exhibit at the Chicago Zoo and landed, unconscious, in the dry moat that separated the gorillas from the gawking humans. A female gorilla called Binti had picked up the boy and carried him to the zookeeper's door, where she waited patiently with the child cradled in the crook of her long, hairy arm. It was this moment the photograph captured. The other gorillas in the exhibit, Alice thought, must have been amazed by the human child that had slipped so suddenly into their midst. Whether they understood the situation or not, they were apparently content to let Binti take charge.

The gorilla-rescues-boy story was compelling, and Alice read it twice, but it was the photograph that held her attention. There was something about the gorilla's posture and the way the light broke over her brow, accentuating the slope of her forehead and filling her eye with a single point of light. And the slight tilt of Binti's solid black head as she looked up at the crowd. The people must have been staring at her in horror. But there was neither harm nor malice in the gorilla's eyes. If Binti could speak she might have told the crowd, "Okay, I've got him, he's safe... what are you waiting for?" But the irony of the photograph was the undeniable reality that one species had come to the aid of another. As she absentmindedly traced Binti's profile with her finger, the message was not lost on Alice. In this small, microcosmic event, a gorilla had guaranteed the survival of a member of a species that had all but wiped her own kind from the face of the earth.

A sudden commotion from the street, a sharp, staccato chorus of children's voices, caused Alice to look up from her magazine. She set down the magazine, walked across the room, cracked open the wooden slats that covered the window, and looked out at the street. A small group of children, the youngest perhaps seven or eight, the oldest no more than thirteen, were harassing a cat. No wait, thought Alice, that's not a cat, it's a gibbon and her baby. A boy chased the young gibbon with a long, sharpened stick, trying to separate it from its mother while an older boy threw rocks at it. The mother gibbon defended her youngster as best she could, attacking first the stone thrower and then the boy with the pointed stick. As the boy with the stick ran, an opportunity was created for the stone thrower. Picking up a broken piece of concrete, he took aim at the baby gibbon, which had stopped to catch its heaving breath. The concrete missile found its mark, hitting the infant squarely in the back of its skull. Two uniformed schoolgirls who were watching from the hood of a parked car laughed and clapped their hands as the baby staggered forward and tumbled into a knee-deep sewer at the side of the road. The mother let out a series of anguished squeaks when she saw her baby lying motionless in the green slime at the bottom of the ditch.

"Hey! Hey!" Alice yelled as she ran out the door, through the rusty gate and into the street. The children's bravado abandoned them when they saw her coming. They dropped their weapons and fled.

The mother gibbon climbed one of the broad-leafed trees that lined the street in this older section of town. She hid herself among the foliage and watched as Alice knelt beside the open sewer. Blood trickled from the nose of the tiny gray corpse and its fine tawny coat was matted with sludge. The infant's brown eyes were open, but the light of life in them had faded. When Alice stepped into the stinking gutter to retrieve the infant, its mother let out a pitiful squeak and retreated farther up the tree. Alice pulled her bandanna from her pocket and wrapped it around the lifeless body, which was no bigger than that of a month-old kitten. From the safety of the tree, the mother gibbon peeked at Alice through her slender gray fingers. Cupping the shrouded body in her hands, Alice looked into the leafy canopy where the gibbon cowered, and shrugged her shoulders helplessly. The mother gibbon watched mutely, silenced by her grief.

Alice wiped her brow on her shirtsleeve, blew a stream of air over her face and tried to collect her thoughts. Her heart pounded and she could not keep her hands from trembling. Finally she turned and carried the infant through the front gate that led to the guesthouse, around the side of the mildew-streaked building and into the back yard, where a dark tangle of fruit trees, shrubs and flowering potted plants grew in botanical disarray. The mother gibbon dropped down from the lowest branch and crept along the ground on all fours, following Alice at a safe distance.

Alice looked around the small yard for a place to bury the baby gibbon. She noticed that shards of jagged glass had been imbedded into the top of the high concrete wall that surrounded the yard. Over there, thought Alice, beneath that fig tree in the corner, that would be a suitable place to lay the little gibbon to rest. She found a trowel near the house and kneeled at the base of the tree.

Scraping away the leaf litter, she exposed the hard yellow clay and started to dig. Fifteen minutes later, exhausted by the heat and the sadness of her task, she finished the grave. She hoped it was deep enough not to be disturbed by any dogs or cats that roamed the neighborhood.

As Alice tamped the dirt with the back of the trowel, the gibbon watched her every move from the safety of a ceramic culvert that connected the guesthouse garden to the adjoining yard. When Alice had finished her task, the gibbon approached warily and sat on her haunches, so close that Alice could have touched her. The gibbon peeled back the corner of Alice's now empty bandanna and peeked under it as if to make sure it no longer concealed her baby. Then the gibbon withdrew and cocked her head, looking at Alice with a puzzled expression. Alice picked up a clump of clay and crumbled it over the grave. The gibbon looked at Alice and then at the grave. She understands, thought Alice, she understands that her baby is dead. While the gibbon watched, Alice continued to crumble clay over the grave until it formed a small mound, which she patted into a slightly elongated shape. She considered marking the grave with a pair of crossed sticks, then thought better of it. The cross was a Christian symbol and Indonesia was primarily a Muslim nation. Instead, Alice decided to mark the grave with three small pebbles. Alice looked at the gibbon, put a finger to her own eye, then traced an imaginary tear down her cheek. "My heart cries," she mouthed silently to the gibbon, pressing her hands over her heart. As the gibbon looked at Alice an expression of understanding filled her dark eyes. Then, to Alice's amazement, the gibbon pointed to her own eye, then crossed her hands over her chest.

As Alice covered the grave with leaves to make it invisible to anyone who might wander through the garden, she heard a faint squeak. She looked up to see the gibbon looking at her from inside the culvert. The gibbon ran through to the other side, then reappeared a moment later. She extended her hand toward Alice, gestured with fingers for Alice to follow, then ducked into the culvert again. Alice crouched down for a better look, peering at the gibbon through the tangled undergrowth. A milky glow of light filled the culvert, but Alice could not make out what was on the other side. Again the gibbon gestured for Alice to follow. Alice felt her scalp tingle and goosepimples rise on her arms as she realized that the gibbon and she were actually communicating. Alice was a courageous girl—sometimes even a little reckless—but this time fear of the unknown, the strangeness of what was happening, and the uncertainty of what waited beyond the arch, kept her rooted in the safety of what was known. She bit her bottom lip and shook her head slowly from side to side, hoping the gibbon would understand that she would not, could not, follow.

The gibbon hopped through the damp leaves, sat on her haunches in front of the kneeling Alice and offered her hand. Again Alice shook her head. "I can't," she whispered. "I have to stay here. My dad told me not to leave, and he'll be back soon." The gibbon slowly unfolded her arms, which seemed extraordinarily long and rubbery to Alice now that the little ape was so close. The gibbon extended her hand and lightly touched Alice at the soft center of her clavicle with her finger. At the moment the gibbon touched her, Alice felt her breath catch. And at that exact moment, Alice felt something within her break away. Filling her mind's eye was an image of a huge chunk of ice breaking off a glacier, floating on its own in deep, uncertain waters. She felt her edges abandon her, leaving her weightless, without form or mass. Her hands were like two helium balloons that wanted to float skyward and it was all she could do to keep them at her side. When the gibbon gestured again for Alice to follow, she surrendered without hesitation. She crawled to the culvert and wiggled through it on her stomach, pulling herself along on her elbows and knees.

On the other side, Alice stood, brushed the dirt from her clothing, and looked around. She was surprised to find that she was not standing in the neighboring yard, but rather in a narrow, cobblestone corridor. Its walls were lined with moss-covered concrete blocks, corrugated tin and plywood. The gibbon scampered ahead and then stopped and looked over her shoulder at Alice, who was walking in a daze, trying to take in her new surroundings. With an open palm, Alice slapped one cheek, then the other. She clapped her hands, wiggled her toes and ran her tongue over her braces. Everything about her seemed as it should, yet she felt different, as if someone had changed her life from one channel to another. Instead of being in the reasonable, comfortable and predictable world she was accustomed to, she was in another slightly skewed, irregular sort of world. And despite the physical evidence to the contrary, she did not feel certain that her body had accompanied her through the culvert and into this new dimension. When she looked back over her shoulder at the narrow alley she had

My dad took this photo of the 'gang' I followed Siti
through on our way to the rain forest. A.S.

just walked through, she thought she saw a girl who looked a lot like her, peering back through the culvert. "Alice," she heard the girl call in a tiny voice something like her own, "don't forget to come back."

"But how will I know to come back if I don't even know where I'm going?" Alice called to the girl.

"Don't worry," said Alice's twin. "You'll know."

Alice waved to the girl, to her former life, then turned to find the gibbon who was perched, waiting patiently, atop a gate made of weathered, paint-splattered boards. Alice realized then that they were in a *gang*, a maze of twisting narrow alleys and passageways that were linked to still more corridors by shallow flights of stairs. When she and her father had visited the ancient city of Chiang Mai in Thailand, she had tried to take a shortcut through a *gang* and ended up lost for hours. That *gang*, like the one she found herself in now, had turned one way then another. If you didn't know your way, it was easy to get lost.

Alice followed the gibbon through the *gang* for what might have been minutes or hours. The watch her father had bought her before they began their trip,

This palm tree at the edge of the forest was full of egrets. A.S.

the one that was supposed to be waterproof to 130 feet, had stopped with both the minute and hour hands pointing straight up, exactly at twelve. She thought vaguely that humidity might be the problem, and that her watch would start up again when she left this muggy, buggy place. But for now, she had neither a watch that worked nor a sense of time.

Alice and the gibbon turned a corner and there in the distance, at the end of a long straightaway, a brilliant patch of emerald green shimmered in the daylight. Both Alice and the gibbon, anxious to escape the claustrophobic confines of the *gang*, ran toward the luxuriant verdant square and stumbled into the sunlight.

They stood at the edge of a sort of buffer zone that separated the city from the forest. It was a work in progress, a strip of dirt choked with weeds and creeping vines and strewn with the putrid, contaminated refuse of human civilization. They picked their way through a sea of empty plastic bags, broken bottles, crushed cardboard boxes, coconut husks and mounds of oil-stained earth and twisted trees recently uprooted by bulldozers. Beyond the debris stood an imposing wall of trees, the edge where the wilderness struggled to hold its own.

Already, some of the exposed trees had begun to dry out, their leaves curled by the heat; their branches were full of egrets.

Apparently feeling vulnerable in the open space, the gibbon scurried across the trash heaps and vanished into the safety of the forest. Alice did her best to keep up, calling, "Wait, wait for me," but the gibbon was already in the tree canopy, using her strong hooked fingers and long arms to swing limb from limb high above the forest floor. A moment later she was just a gray dust mote among the leaves.

"Where are you?" called Alice, stumbling along in the forest now, her eyes scanning the foliage above her.

The gibbon leaped onto a limb, squeaked urgently, then brachiated through the canopy like a trapeze artist.

With her eyes skyward, Alice stumbled along a rough trail until she came to a shoulder-wide wooden catwalk which crossed a swamp of what looked like strong murky tea. Trying not to think about what might be lurking beneath the surface of the amber water, she swallowed hard and, holding her arms out for balance, started across the narrow catwalk. The increase in humidity was striking as Alice made her way across the swamp. She had to breathe deeply to fill her lungs with oxygen.

The gibbon was waiting for her when she reached the other side. "Where are we going?" Alice said beneath her breath.

"To the village," answered the gibbon, with a whooping call that entered Alice's mind as words she could understand.

Alice stopped in her tracks. "I... I just heard you," she said, covering her ears. "In my head—just like you were... talking to me."

"I *am* talking to you," said the gibbon.

"But why am I just now understanding you, when before all I heard were squeaks?"

"I don't know," said the gibbon, and Alice thought she saw the little ape shrug. "Maybe it's because we're in the forest now."

"Why would that make a difference?"

"The forest has a way of sharpening your senses," the gibbon said.

"Well, yes, I suppose it does," said Alice, suddenly aware of the trills and chirps of insects and birds all around her, and the far off whoop-whoop of other gibbons. She couldn't hear the city any more. No motorcycles, no honking horns.

The two of them—the teenage girl running along the trail and the gibbon swinging through the canopy above—made an odd pair as they worked their way through a forest that became denser and darker with each step. "Do you have a name?" shouted Alice, looking up into the canopy.

"Siti," said the gibbon.

"Well, Siti, why are we going to the village?"

"Because we need your help."

CHAPTER TWO

Stranger in a Strange Land

A mosquito net hung like a tired ghost over Shane Bailey's narrow bed. Through the milky gauze he watched a translucent white gecko, no longer than his thumb, climb the wooden wall with half a cricket sticking out of its mouth. The insect's legs were still pumping like a deranged fiddler. It was another hot Saturday on the equator and Shane was a long way from home, feeling as sorry for himself as he felt for the doomed cricket.

Shane's room, which hung like an unpainted afterthought off the back of a Pepto-Bismol-pink house , was not quite finished. In one corner of the eight-by-ten foot cubicle stood a homemade wooden desk with one leg shorter than the other three. A few papers lay scattered on its rough-hewn surface along with an Indonesian-English dictionary, gathering dust next to a lamp that sometimes worked. Above the lamp a small window overlooked a backyard of overgrown tropical foliage and an outdoor toilet that was connected to the kitchen at the back of the house by a rickety wooden catwalk.

Shane's jeans, shirt and San Francisco Giants baseball cap hung limply from rusty nails driven into an exposed stud near the door. The rest of his clothes he kept in two baskets at the foot of his bed, one for clean, one for soiled. A 40-

watt bulb dangled from a thin wire at the center of the room and a single electrical outlet stared out from the wall, near his desk. To charge his laptop computer, or occasionally to shave the fuzz that had recently started to sprout from his chin, Shane had to unplug his desk lamp.

A mosquito whined past Shane's ear and he sat up quickly, entangling his head in the low-hanging mosquito net while slapping the insect away with his hands, which also became enmeshed in the net. Freeing himself, he rose from the bed, picked up the spray bottle of insect repellent on the table and held the bill of his baseball cap in front of his pale blue eyes. He misted his face and blond hair liberally with the poison. Shane found a lot of things about Indonesia not to his liking, but nothing was quite as irritating to him as the incessant mosquito attacks.

Shane had not expected his life as an American foreign exchange student to be like this. The brochure from the Student Exchange office, with its color photographs of happy families engaged in conversation around dinner tables, bore little resemblance to the reality of his life here in Indonesian Borneo. He thought about Vincent, the French student who had stayed with him and his grandmother one summer in California. His grandmother had taken Vincent and him to San Francisco, where they stayed in a fancy hotel and sat behind home plate at a Giants game. Afterwards they took a cab to NikeTown and Shane's grandmother bought each of them hundred-dollar sneakers—which might have been made right here in Indonesia by workers making twenty dollars a month. Shane wondered idly, as he felt the perspiration trickle down his neck, where the photographs of the nice neat families in those fancy houses in the brochure had been taken. Switzerland? Germany? How about that photograph of the boy sitting at a well-lighted desk in an elegantly furnished room? Where was that photo taken? Spain? The Netherlands? He knew for certain that it was not taken in this little East Kalimantan village, where he was destined to ride out the remainder of the school year like a passenger on a bus to the middle of nowhere.

Shane didn't know exactly what he had expected of Borneo, but it certainly was not this rickety house where the outside walls and the inside walls were the same wall. In his wildest dreams he had not expected to be living with a cab driver's family on the outskirts of Balikpapan. Didn't the people in the Student

Exchange office investigate these places before they dispatched innocent and unsuspecting students like Shane to the frayed split ends of the earth? Didn't these families somehow have to qualify? Wasn't there some sort of minimum standard that had to be met?

Though Shane didn't know for certain, he suspected that the financial incentive for an Indonesian family to take a foreign exchange student into their household was very tempting. Host families received several hundred dollars each month for the support of the student. That was more than many Indonesian families spent on food in an entire year. There was no way that all that money was spent on him. What's a meal cost in East Kalimantan? Fifty cents? Seventy-five? And that's if you ate in the mom-and-pop restaurants along the main road. His host family seldom took him out for a meal. He ate rice and noodles, noodles and rice (sometimes with a few mystery vegetables stirred into the mix), three times a day. Occasionally there was peanut sauce (which he liked) or some salty tempe (pressed bean cake, which he didn't like), or a shark's head floating in broth. Oh well, what did he expect, a McDonald's on the corner? There were no familiar fast-food restaurants in this corner of the world, at least not yet.

The fact was that Shane's unhappiness and self-pity had nothing to do with the house he was living in, or the family he was living with, or how his adoptive family treated him. His Indonesian hosts were friendly and cordial and treated him like one of their family. The problem was that Shane didn't want to be part of this or any other exchange family, no matter how well he was treated. He wanted his own family. He wanted his own mom and dad, his own brothers, his own room, his own friends, his own school in his own rural California community. And he missed his own culture more than he'd known it possible to miss something of which he'd barely been aware. By now, after toughing it out in Indonesia for two months, Shane had arrived at the conclusion that there was no point in his going to school in Indonesia. He wasn't learning anything here. How could he? He didn't understand a word his teachers said. There was absolutely nothing for him to learn here, nothing. As far as Shane was concerned, the entire bug-infested country had little to offer him and each passing day was a day of his youth wasted, a day he would never get back.

What Shane really longed to do was take a shower, a real shower, and wash away the sweat and grit and insect repellent once and for all. He'd had enough

This is the house I lived in as a foreign exchange student in Borneo. My bedroom was around the back. S.B.

of standing in a dark, damp wooden room, no bigger than a closet, pouring scoops of lukewarm water over himself from a plastic tub. And he wanted to use a toilet that flushed, not one that you had to pour water down to clear. He wanted to be able to flick the handle and be done with it. And he longed to put his mouth under a faucet and feel cool clean mountain water trickle down his throat, water that was not a conduit for bacteria and viruses which preyed upon his delicate digestive tract and left him with constant diarrhea. At home, not once in his sixteen years had he wondered if the water he drank was safe. He'd never given it a thought, but now it was all he thought about. He was tired of walking around with an emergency wad of toilet paper and extra skivvies stuffed in his backpack, the contents of which he thought of as his Indonesian survival kit.

Shane longed to play baseball and football again, instead of badminton, soccer and table tennis. He daydreamed about catching the pass that won the game and brought the crowd to its feet and the cheerleaders, with their perfect teeth and rustling blue-and-gold pom-poms, to his side. He wanted to listen to rock music, and he wanted to read the sports pages of the newspaper. He didn't even

WHAT THE ORANGUTAN TOLD ALICE

Indonesian teenagers love to play volleyball. The guy giving me
the thumbs-up here is my host brother, Adi. S.B.

know how his beloved 49ers were doing. There was no news here, at least none
that he cared about, just some rumblings from discontented people on a far-away
island in this nation of islands. He sighed deeply and brushed a stray tear from
his eye. God, he was homesick.

It wasn't that the Indonesians weren't friendly to Shane. They were extreme-
ly cordial, and always greeted him with a smile and a respectful "Good morning,
Mr. Shane." But friendliness and smiling faces were not substitutes for good conversation. The language barrier isolated him; he might as well be deaf and mute.
No matter how hard he tried to learn Indonesian, or how often he referred to his
phrase book (which wasn't often enough), the language eluded him, like a butterfly flittering just out of reach. And most Indonesians did not speak English,
or at least not very much English. Certainly no one in his host family had much
command of Shane's native tongue. Oh, his host-brother Adi knew a few words
and phrases, and the two of them did manage to have some simple conversa-
tions, but nothing with any depth. It wasn't as if they could have a normal
conversation about baseball or girls. Most Indonesians knew how to say "hello,

mister,'" and "good morning" and "hello, how are you?," but that was about the extent of it. Try to have a meaningful conversation in English and you could see their dark eyes glaze over. English was as foreign to the Indonesians as Indonesian was to Shane.

But deep down, Shane knew he had not made an honest effort to adapt to the Indonesian way of life. And he knew, too, that he probably was not the best candidate for the student exchange program. His romantic notion of spending a year away from his bickering parents just did not mesh with the reality of living in a fragmented nation that was mostly water and spread out over some 17,000 islands. The hard truth was that he was not prepared for this kind of life. He lacked the adaptability and imagination required of students studying abroad; he couldn't, or wouldn't, adjust to the change. But when he e-mailed his parents from the Internet cafe in downtown Balikpapan, he blamed his unhappiness on the Indonesians. He made it sound as if they had not accommodated him, had somehow failed him and made him feel unwelcome. He was hoping his parents would feel guilty and stop fighting long enough to bring him home. But he'd given up hope that would ever happen.

Shane slipped his feet into his sneakers and tied the laces with a double bow. He checked the contents of his backpack for items he had learned never to leave home without. In unpredictable Indonesia, you never knew what turns your day would take. Okay, thought Shane, running through the checklist he had committed to memory: bottled water, Powerbars, sunscreen, roll of toilet paper (can't go anywhere, literally, without toilet paper), insect repellent, Gerber pocket tool, compass, sunglasses, headlamp, the old Nikon camera his grandfather had given him for recording his adventures, a couple of rolls of film, Imodium and an extra pair of shorts. Okay, that should about cover it. Hoisting the bag over his shoulder, he left the house and stepped into the blazing equatorial sun.

Almost immediately, a shine of perspiration covered his too-pale skin. By the time he reached the front gate his long-sleeved T-shirt clung to his body. The unpaved road that Shane plodded along divided the village into equal halves. Most of the small businesses and nicer houses were clustered at the center of the village. The subsistence farmers, who coaxed their livelihoods from the nutrient-poor soil, lived in small houses on small plots of land at the edge of town. Shane stopped at a tiny storefront that was part of somebody's house and that had everything from toothpaste to kerosene mingling on its dusty, sagging shelves, and bought a bunch of small, ripe, sweet-tasting bananas that were native to the South American continent and now thrived in this part of the world. He continued his walk along the potholed street, past the village motorcycle repair shop with its skeletons of scooters leaning against the outside wall and its wooden crates of oily parts stacked inside. Next to the motorcycle shop was the thatched ojek lean-to where motorcycle taxi drivers played card dominos in the shade as they waited for fares. A flock of scrawny chickens scratching in the dust squawked and scattered as he strolled toward the elementary school with its open windows and dusty playground. In spite of the heat and humidity, a volleyball game was in progress in the yard. When Adi spotted Shane, he invited him to join the game. "Too hot," said Shane, fanning his face with his hand, a gesture that once again isolated him from the community that did its best to include him. Shane pulled his camera from his backpack and took a photo of the game, and then walked between two buildings toward the back of the school, amazed at how the Indonesians could be so oblivious to the intense tropical heat.

Though Shane did not have many friends in the village, he did have one. With this friend, language was not a barrier. His friend was a long-armed Mueller's gibbon who lived at the end of a chain behind the elementary school, serving time for the sin of survival. The gibbon had regularly raided a garden at the edge of the village until the morning he was snared by a farmer who was cleverer than the gibbon was cautious. In an effort to spare the gibbon's life, one of the elementary school teachers had suggested that the small ape be kept as a pet for the school children. Perhaps, suggested the teacher, the children could study its behavior. And so it was that the gibbon, whom the children named Berani and who, until his capture, had moved as lightly as the breeze through the forest canopy, came to live as a prisoner at the back of the elementary school.

Shane felt sorry for the gibbon from the moment his host-brother Adi proudly showed him the school children's pet.

"But Adi, what kind of life is this for him, chained up all day?" Shane had asked, looking at the gibbon's forlorn dark eyes peering at him from within the white wreath of fur that surrounded its face.

"His life is not so bad," Adi had said. "The children pay attention to him and give him food. Besides, what does it matter, it's only a monkey."

"But isn't it illegal to keep a gibbon as a pet?" Shane had said, thinking he had read something about this.

"No one cares, the law is not enforced," Adi had said.

Shane had recognized this conversation as a cultural barrier between his host-brother and himself and thought it best not to pursue a discussion about the treatment of animals, especially since he was newly arrived and wanted to make as good an impression as possible. But as he looked at the gibbon that first day, and at the elements that defined its dismal life—the empty water dish, the flies buzzing around the scraps in his food bowl, the chafed skin at his neck—he vowed to do what he could to improve the small primate's life. As the school year progressed, and as Shane became increasingly homesick and unhappy with his life in the village, he spent more and more of his free time with Berani the gibbon.

"Why do you like that monkey so much?" Adi asked him one day as they walked home from school.

"I don't know, I just do" Shane answered, reluctant to admit that he felt sorry for the gibbon. "And, besides, he's an ape, not a monkey."

"Ape, monkey, what's the difference?" said Adi.

"Well, for one thing, apes don't have tails," said Shane.

Over time, Shane began to feel that the gibbon and he were two of a kind, kindred spirits held against their wills and yearning for the lives they'd lost.

"Hey, bud," said Shane as he approached the gibbon, who was sitting in a narrow blade of shade cast by the overhanging roof of the school. "You doing okay? I brought you some bananas. I'll get you some fresh water." The curious gibbon examined a banana carefully, then peeled and ate the fruit just as a human would.

Shane squatted on his heels Indonesian style and took a photograph of his poor little friend. He extended a hand and the little ape wrapped his bony gray fingers around Shane's index finger. "One of these days we're getting out of here," Shane promised the gibbon. The gibbon cocked his head as if trying to understand what Shane was telling him. "I don't know how and I don't know when, but one of these days we'll both be back where we belong." The gibbon looked at Shane, hiccuped a mournful squeak, then reached for another banana.

Emotional Rescue

A t the edge of the forest, Alice crouched behind an eight-foot high, lichen-covered buttress, one of several fin-like growths that helped stabilize the shallow-rooted dipterocarp tree that towered sixty feet over her head. Above, hidden in a tangle of broad, leathery leaves, Siti sat and absentmindedly scratched her ribcage as she peered across the clearing to the schoolyard. Alice peeked over the buttress at the slender blond boy who was kneeling in the dirt, feeding bananas to a pathetic-looking gibbon who was chained to a stake.

"No children around," whispered Siti, shaking a leafy branch. "It must be one of the days when they don't come here."

"Is that gibbon a friend of yours?"

"That's Yayat, my poor sweet Yayat," said Siti. "My mate."

"Your mate?" said Alice. "Oh, now I get it. Who's that boy?"

"I don't know his name, but he comes every day to give Yayat bananas and fresh water. He made a little shelter out of some old boards and palm leaves so Yayat could have some shade and get out of the rain. He has been very kind to my Yayat."

"He's kind of cute," mused Alice, as she watched Shane.

"He has a good heart, for a twoleg," said Siti.

"Well, let's go say hello," said Alice, looking to Siti to see if the gibbon thought her suggestion was a good one.

When Shane saw the blonde girl and the small gray gibbon emerge from the edge of the rain forest, he thought the Borneo heat had finally gotten to him. He watched as Siti scampered over to the captive gibbon, who was straining at his chain excitedly pawing the air.

"Hi, I'm Alice," said Alice, offering her hand.

Shane could not believe his eyes. Who was this girl, and what was she doing here? "Howdy," he said finally, shaking Alice's hand. "I'm Shane, Shane Bailey."

"Nice to meet you, Shane," said Alice. "This is Siti, Yayat's mate. She told me all about what happened to Yayat."

"Yayat? You mean Berani?"

"Berani? Is that what the kids named him? Siti told me his name is Yayat."

Shane took off his cap and used his forearm to wipe the sweat from his brow. "Dang, it's hot today, isn't it?"

"The humidity must be ninety percent," said Alice.

"Looks like it might rain."

"Yeah," said Alice, turning her gaze to the dark clouds rolling across the sky. "Could happen."

Shane watched Siti as she kneaded the back of the gibbon formerly known as Berani with her thin, backscratcher fingers searching for parasites. "What do you mean, she told you about Yayat?"

"Well, I know it'll sound weird, and you're probably going to think I'm crazy, but something strange happened when I went into the forest with Siti. I can't explain it exactly, but I can, like, actually understand Siti and... she can understand me."

"Are you trying to tell me that you and Siti actually... talk?"

Alice nodded and Shane laughed. "You've got to be from California, right?"

"How did you know?"

"I can spot 'em a mile away."

"But that doesn't mean I'm a kook," said Alice.

"Hey, don't worry about it, I'm from California, too."

Alice felt somewhat dismayed that Shane was not taking her revelation seriously. "Hey look, if you don't believe that Siti and I can communicate, fine, that's up to you. Let's just figure out how we're going to get Yayat out of the mess he's in, okay?"

"Cool," said Shane. "I'm all for that."

Alice knelt in the dust and examined the small padlock that held the chain around Yayat's neck. "Geez, no collar. Look, the chain's rubbed him raw."

"I've been putting antibiotic cream on him," said Shane with a sigh. "I've been lobbying for a leather collar, but no one seems to care."

"Why didn't you just do it?" asked Alice.

Shane shrugged. "Didn't want to make waves, I guess."

"Well, the first thing we've got to do is get this stupid lock off," said Alice. "Do you know where the key is?"

"Nope," said Shane.

"Hmmm," said Alice.

"I've got an idea," said Shane, examining the padlock as he was slowly drawn into the conspiracy to set Yayat free. "I've got a lock back at the house that kind of looks like this one. Maybe I can borrow a bolt cutter from the motorcycle shop, cut this padlock, set Yayat free, and then replace this lock with mine. I doubt that anyone would notice that the lock's been switched. If anyone asks what happened, I'll say Berani wasn't getting enough food and his head shrank."

"His head shrank?" said Alice.

"This is Borneo," said Shane. "The land of shrunken heads."

"Gross."

"Everyone will think he just wiggled out of it."

"The Great Lock Switch," said Alice, nodding her head approvingly. "I think it's a good plan. Let's go for it."

"You guys wait here," said Shane. "I'll be right back."

"Don't you think someone might see us?" said Alice, paranoid now that she had committed herself to a crime.

"Naw, everyone's either playing volleyball or watching the ping pong match on television. No one hangs out here on weekends."

Fifteen minutes later, Shane was back. "The motorcycle repair shop was closed," said Shane, unzipping his backpack and removing a padlock and a pair of bolt cutters, "but the door wasn't."

"Pretty bold move," said Alice.

"I guess sometimes you gotta do what you gotta do," said Shane, kneeling beside his gibbon friend. "Hold still Yayat, this won't hurt a bit."

With Alice holding the bolt-cutter blades on the lock, Shane squeezed the handles. The metal ring of the lock snapped like a thin stalk of bamboo and the chain fell away from Yayat's neck.

"All right!" said Shane.

"Freedom!" said Alice.

The two gibbons scampered gleefully around in a circle, then scurried for the sanctuary of the forest. They leaped into the nearest tree as if gravity were a force that applied to everything on earth except them. Then Siti stopped on a low branch and beckoned at Alice and Shane to follow.

Alice took a couple of steps, then turned to Shane. "You coming?"

"What? Into the forest?" said Shane, raising his eyebrows.

"Sure," said Alice. "Why not?"

Shane shook his head doubtfully and stared at the ground, nudging the dust with his shoe. "I don't know, the rain forest makes me kind of, you know, nervous or something."

"Nervous?"

"Yeah, all the snakes and bugs and stuff—it's downright dangerous in there. I mean, I really like nature and everything, but I'd rather watch it on the Discovery Channel, where it can't bite me."

Alice laughed and lifted her ponytail off her neck. "That's television, Shane, not nature. Come on, where's your sense of adventure?" Geez, she thought, isn't that what her dad asked her just a couple of weeks ago?

Shane sighed and felt his last bit of resistance evaporate under Alice's steady gaze. "Oh, all right, but we have to be back by dark, okay?"

"Sure, whatever," said Alice, tapping her watch, the hands of which still had not moved. "Siti? Yayat?" she called, jogging into the forest with Shane close behind. "Where'd you guys go?"

Siti's chatter drifted down from the canopy. "Up here, Alice. Yayat's found some figs."

I took this photo of Yayat just after Alice and I liberated him
with the bolt cutter. S.B.

Shane suddenly covered his ears with his hands. "Dang! I heard that," he said. "Like an echo or something."

"See, I told you. It's happening to you, too," said Alice. "And you know what else is weird?"

"What?" said Shane, not sure he wanted to know.

"There's no time here."

"No time?" said Shane. "What do you mean, there's no time?"

"There's no time. We're just stuck in the moment," Alice explained. "There's no future, no past, only right now, right here."

"Hey, girl, that's not possible."

"Well, I admit it's strange, but it is possible," said Alice. "Look, over there at the school, what do you see?"

Shane shaded his eyes with his hand and peered through the undergrowth at the edge of the forest. Astonished, he watched himself put a padlock on the chain, pick up the bolt cutter and run as fast as his legs would carry him between two buildings.

"What the—what the heck is going on here, instant replay?" said Shane, looking at Alice in bewilderment. "How'd you do that?"

Alice laughed. "I didn't do anything."

"Well, something weird is going on," said Shane. "What do we do now?"

"Well, we can either go home and watch the ping-pong game on television, or stay with what's happening here and see where it takes us," said Alice matter-of-factly. She sounded braver than she actually felt.

Shane took off his cap and scratched his head. "I don't know...."

"What's the matter, are you chicken?"

"Of course not," said Shane indignantly, deciding then and there that he would not have his courage challenged by this rambunctious California girl who was, after all, younger than he was. He cleared his throat. "Okay, what are we waiting for. Let's go."

"You can go back any time you want," Yayat said from the canopy, his mouth full of juicy figs.

"But there's someone in the forest we want you to meet," said Siti.

Shane drew a deep breath and exhaled slowly. "You know, they don't play these kinds of games back home," he said to no one in particular.

"Who?" Alice said to Siti. "Who do you want us to meet?"

"The Old Man," said Siti.

"The old man?" said Shane. "What old man?"

"The Old Man of the Forest," answered Siti.

Yayat dropped down from the canopy, a bright orange smear of fig on his dark face. He wrapped his fingers around Shane's left index finger and looked up at him. "Thank you, my friend, for taking care of me while I was a captive, and for keeping your promise to set me free. Now it's my turn."

"Your turn to what?" asked Shane.

"To set you free," said Yayat.

CHAPTER 4

Batman and the Hornbill

I t wouldn't be fair to say that Nik was a lazy orangutan. It was just that he didn't want to travel any farther for his first meal of the day than was absolutely necessary. With this in mind, he selected as the site for his night's nest the top branches of an ulin tree that grew next to a Sindora wallichii. An abundance of spine-covered pods, tasty fruit that would provide Nik with a nutritious meal, dangled temptingly from the limbs of the sindora.

These days Nik had to choose his nest sites carefully. No longer a lanky, lightweight juvenile who could build a nest just about anywhere he pleased and feel secure, Nik was now an eleven-year-old subadult, and was starting to develop the bulky, muscular body of an adult orangutan. His nest had to be strong enough to support his hundred-pound body. Though he'd never admit it, Nik had a touch of acrophobia; he was afraid of heights. His personal history was such that he had not developed the intuitive climbing skills of his forest-raised kin, who had spent most of their lives in the canopy. But with each passing day, Nik's tree-climbing skills and judgement improved. Lately his errors in judgement were few and far between.

Nik selected a spot on the ulin tree where a thick limb extended out from the trunk parallel to the forest floor. Squatting on the limb, he bounced up and down to test its strength. Satisfied that he had chosen wisely, he sat on a branch that sprouted from the limb and began to wrap smaller sprouting branches around his body, tucking them under the branch on which he squatted. He repeated this procedure five or six times. Then he tore off some small branches and leaves within his reach and tucked them between his body and the woody framework of his nest. While Nik didn't actually weave his nest as did a bird, or as his chimpanzee kin in Africa were sometimes known to do, he did tamp the leafy branches into place and tuck an occasional errant but resilient twig under a more stable limb to hold it in place. This wasn't weaving, technically, but it was close. Nik pulled himself out of the nest and retrieved a few more leafy branches for padding. From his nest, the view of the treetops in the golden light of morning would be nothing short of spectacular. He grunted approvingly.

Nik bounced in his nest one final time to test its strength and comfort level. After all, he would be here from dusk until dawn and, like any snoozing crea-ture, he wanted to be as comfortable as possible. Not bad, he thought, tearing off a leafy branch or two for use as a blanket or an umbrella, in case the tropical night turned cool or rainy. He curled his long fingers around the branch that provided the main support for his nest, and left them there. If during the night he tossed and turned, his grip on the ulin branch would tighten reflexively and prevent his fall to the forest floor. Nik yawned, exposing his full complement of yellowish teeth, including his pair of four-inch incisors, and promptly dozed off to the monotonous lullaby of a pair of Indian cuckoos nesting in the forest understory somewhere in the distance. In his drowsy state, the song of the cuck-oos recalled to him his youth, and memories of the four-note scales that a little girl played on her wooden recorder in the human household he'd lived in a long, long time ago.

Twelve hours later the dark night sky yielded to a pale-orange slice of light on the horizon. The nocturnal animals that had been prowling the forest in search of food—the slow lories, tarsiers, fruit bats, civets and clouded leopards—made their way back to the sanctuaries of their daytime nests.

The sounds of the forest coming awake nudged Nik from his dream-filled sleep. First there was the occasional chirp-chirp of a cricket. Then, as the sun broke through the cloud cover, a cicada started to vibrate with its distinctive electric buzz. Then another cicada chimed in, then another and another until the whirling hurricane of cicada racket woke the Indian cuckoos, who then harmonized with their own four-note melody. The last song to join the chorus was the clear territorial call of the resident gibbons. One started with a "*whoop, whoop, whoop*" that rose higher and higher, building to a full-throated, bubbling crescendo that is one of the sweetest and most memorable melodies to be heard anywhere on earth. Then, from miles away, another gibbon chimed in with its call, establishing its territory for all within earshot. And then from even farther away another gibbon made its declaration of rain forest real estate. The symphony spread through the still morning forest like a drop of ink in a glass of clear water.

Nik stirred in his nest. He yawned widely, smacked his rubbery lips and emitted a tentative little kiss-squeak. He stretched and felt a rumbling deep in his bowels: he was hungry. He turned his attention to the neighboring sindora tree's fruit, glistening just out of reach in the morning sun. He climbed halfway down the ulin tree until he could reach the branches of a slender diospyros growing nearby. He pulled the branches toward him until the diospyros trunk was close enough that he could make a graceful transition from one tree to the other. As Nik climbed the trunk it started to bend under his weight. He climbed a few feet higher and the tree trunk gave even more. Then he started to rock back and forth, causing the damp leaves and branches to rustle in the crisp morning air. The higher Nik climbed, the more the tree swayed under his weight. When the arc of the diospyros carried him far enough toward the sindora, Nik reached out, grabbed a sturdy limb, let go of the diospyros, and suddenly found himself in the fruit-laden sindora, where he wanted to be. The entire process was the orangutan equivalent of a person leaving his house in the morning and walking to the café down the street for breakfast.

Nik focused his attention on the pods of sindora fruit as he walked up the tree, wrapping his hooked fingers around the trunk. The long toes and soles of his feet pressed against the trunk for additional support. A few moments later he moved to a branch that led to the legume buffet. Holding a limb with each foot so that no single branch bore his entire weight, Nik hung upside down like a bat. With his hands now free, he began to pick the leathery, spine-covered pods, tearing them open to get at the pea-like seeds inside. He spit out the black seeds, which fell like pebbles to the forest floor. Some of the seeds would germinate where they landed and the stronger ones would sprout into saplings, which would compete with other plants for the nutrients and sunlight that would help them grow. Other seeds would become meals for the birds and rodents that scoured the understory for food. These seeds would eventually be deposited elsewhere, miraculously pre-fertilized by their journey through the bird's or rodent's digestive tract, to sprout and grow into more sindora trees.

A rhinoceros hornbill, a gawky cartoon of a bird, appeared over the canopy where Nik now dined. A pair of long white tail feathers trailed like party streamers behind his black body. The hornbill's strong, broad wings ripped through the atmosphere with short, choppy strokes that generated a powerful whoosh, whoosh, whoosh as they beat the calm morning air to invisible shreds. The hornbill's yellow eyes rotated forward in their sockets, peering down the length of his eighteen-inch-long, red-orange bill at the crowns of green trees that stretched endlessly before him like a forest of broccoli blooms basking in the buttery sunlight of a new day.

"Hello, Nik," the hornbill called when he saw the acrobatic orangutan hanging upside down in the sindora tree.

Nik looked up past his red, hairy toes at the hornbill gliding through the sky, which was slightly scented these days with the smoky stench of faraway fires. "Hello yourself, Sarijan," Nik grunted as the bird flew past.

Through a break in the canopy, Sarijan spied a pair of gibbons brachiating through the trees and below them, an unmatched pair of twolegs hiking along the narrow trail. His curiosity piqued, he settled onto a branch and hid behind a spray of leaves until the gibbons were within shouting, or in Sarijan's case, cackling distance.

"Psssst. Hey Siti, Yayat," Sarijan cackled to the gibbons. "What's with those twolegs down there?"

"They're friends of ours," said Siti, looking up into the canopy but unable to see the hornbill. "Good twolegs."

"Is there such a thing?" answered Sarijan, hopping into view.

"They helped me escape from the village," said Yayat.

"And the girl, she tried to save my baby," said Siti, a sad drift to her voice.

"We're going to take them to meet the Old Man," said Yayat.

"If we can find him," added Siti.

"You'll only find the Old Man if he wants to be found," said Sarijan. "Maybe Nik can help you."

"Nik?" said Yayat. "I haven't seen Nik in a civet's age. I thought he'd moved on."

"I just saw him," said Sarijan. "He's hanging upside down in a sindora tree just off the trail. He looks like a bat without wings. You can't miss him."

"Thanks," said Siti.

"Do you want to meet our twolegged friends?" Yayat called to Sarijan.

"I don't know," said Sarijan. "I don't much trust twolegs, you know."

"I know," said Siti. "I was so sorry to hear Suci had been... you know... harvested."

"Harvested?" said Sarijan. "That's just another word for murder."

"Why someone would kill her just to take her tail feathers is completely beyond my comprehension," said Yayat, scratching the fringe of white hair that surrounded his face.

"Makes no sense," agreed Siti.

"All right, I'll hop down for a quick howdy, but let me have some fun with them first," said Sarijan. Stretching out his red, featherless neck, he let out a long, loud, cackling call that sounded amplified, like someone twisting dry wheat stalks in front of a microphone. Then he made his voice rise suddenly in pitch and volume. It evolved into loud, maniacal, horror-movie laughter that would frighten any human out of their wits.

"What is that?" said Alice, scanning the canopy in fear. She turned to Shane, her eyebrows arching like question marks over her wide-open brown eyes.

"I don't know," gulped Shane, his voice suddenly rising an octave. "I'm not sure I want to find out, either. It sounds like a crazy person loose up in the trees somewhere."

Siti dropped down to the forest floor. "It's only Sarijan, our rhinoceros hornbill friend," she explained to Alice and Shane. "He likes to scare people with his call."

"Well, he sure as heck is doing a good job of it," said Shane, his voice dropping back to normal as he brushed a mosquito away from his ear. "Scared poor Alice here half to death."

"No offense intended," said Sarijan.

Alice, who knew about parrots but had never seen even a photograph of a hornbill, could not take her eyes from the extraordinary bird. Growing out the top of Sarijan's beak, close to his yellow eyes, was a large, bright orange bony growth, flat on top, a kind of a horn that appeared to be part of its skull.

"What're you staring at, honey," said Sarijan. "Never seen a hornbill before?"

"I'm sorry," said Alice. "It's just that you're so... unusual looking."

"No more so than you, my dear," replied Sarijan.

"What do you use that, that..."

"Casque," said Sarijan. "I use it, well, I used it, to tamp mud into my mate's nest, to seal it off while she sat on her eggs."

"Looks like a dang horn to me," said Shane.

"Duh," said Sarijan. "Hey, that's probably why they call me a hornbill!"

"You'll have to excuse Sarijan," said Siti. "He's really very nice, but he's recently had an unfortunate experience with a twoleg."

"Unfortunate experience? You call watching your mate take a dart an 'unfortunate experience'?" scolded Sarijan. He ruffled his body feathers indignantly and said, "I'm outta here."

"Wait," said Shane. "Can I take a picture of you before you leave?"

"A picture?" said Sarijan. "Why?"

"Because I want to remember you, and what you looked like."

"Well," said Sarijan, a little flattered. No one had ever taken his photograph before. "I guess one wouldn't hurt. Where do you want me?"

"Maybe if you could just perch on this branch over here," suggested Shane, pointing to a nearby branch that was about at his eye level.

Sarijan fluttered down so that he was just a yard or two from Shane. "I think my left profile is my best, don't you?"

"I don't know," said Shane. "Alice, what do you think?"

Alice put her hand to her chin and considered as Sarijan turned his head from side to side. "It's definitely a close call," she said, "but I'd have to agree with Sarijan, the left side is better."

"That's what I said," said Sarijan.

Shane brought Sarijan into focus in the Nikon's viewfinder. "There, right there, hold it."

Sarijan the hornbill was one cool-looking bird. S.B.

Ka-plop went the shutter.

"Oh man, that was perfect," said Shane.

"Are you through?" said Sarijan.

"I think so," said Shane. "Thanks, thanks a lot."

The huge bird then spread his wings, jumped into the air and flew up and through a small opening in the dense tree canopy. "Good luck with the Old Man," he yelled as he vanished into the darkening haze, "if you can find him." Alice, Shane and the gibbons listened as the hornbill's maniacal laughter faded in the distance.

"That's what I call a bird with an attitude," said Alice.

"Can't really blame him, though," said Yayat.

"Seems like all of us forest dwellers have had unpleasant experiences with twolegs," said Siti sadly.

"Well, enough of this chit-chat," said Yayat. "Let's see if we can find old Nik."

A Nik of Time

Are you sure they're harmless?" Nik asked Yayat, his hairy red arms wrapped around a tree trunk like stripes around a barber's pole. From where Yayat and Nik sat high in the sindora tree, Alice and Shane looked like one of the 30,000 species of beetles that called Borneo home.

"Of course I'm sure," said Yayat. "I told you, they rescued me from a life of captivity, and the girl, Alice, she helped Siti when the twoleg children attacked our baby."

"That kid with the backpack," said Nik, eyeing Shane suspiciously. "What makes you so sure he doesn't have a slingshot stashed in there?"

"Naw, I'd bet my tail he doesn't," Yayat assured Nik.

"You don't have a tail," said Nik.

"Of course I don't have a tail—I'm an ape. But if I did have one I'd bet every inch of it that Shane's not packing a slingshot," said Yayat. "Come on, Nik, let's go down so you can meet them. Maybe you can take them to meet the Old Man. What do you say?"

"The Old Man?" said Nik. "You want me to take them to meet the Old Man?"

"I think these kids could learn a lot from the Old Man," said Yayat. "And with the way things are going, we need as many twolegs on our side as possible."

Nik scratched his chin thoughtfully and nodded. "Yes, that's very true. There's not much time left."

"Just come down and talk to them. What have you got to lose? You'll see, they may be young twolegs, but they are good ones."

Nik wrapped his hooked fingers around the sindora trunk and walked down it as easily as if the tree were a log lying flat on the forest floor. Yayat followed like a shadow.

"Alice and Shane, this is our friend Nik," said Siti when Nik and Yayat had reached the forest floor. She reached up to touch the orangutan's arm. "Nik, say hello to Alice and Shane."

"I'm pleased to meet you," said Shane, tentatively extending his hand to the orangutan, who squatted in the leaf litter on the forest floor. When Nik showed no interest in shaking it, Shane shoved his hand deep in the pocket of his jeans. Looking at the size of Nik's hands, easily three or four times bigger than his own, Shane thought it was just as well the orangutan didn't want to shake.

Until now, Shane had only seen orangutans in zoos, and always at a distance, across a moat or some other separation barrier. He was amazed at how different an orangutan looked up close. Nik's face was big, with a forehead that sloped back from his heavy brow and cast a shadow over his small, close-set amber eyes. There was something familiar in the orangutan's eyes, Shane thought. They were not like a dog's eyes, or a cat's, or the eyes of any other animal he knew. Surrounded by a circle of soft, peach-colored skin and full of expression and depth, Nik's eyes were more like human eyes.

Shane remembered the camera in his backpack. "Nik, is it okay if I take a picture of you?"

Nik shrugged indifferently and grunted. Shane didn't know whether that was a yes or a no, so he took a chance and snapped a quick photo anyway. "Dang," said Shane, disappointed at what a slow shutter speed was necessary. "Not much light in the forest, is there?"

The top of Nik's head was covered with short, reddish-brown hair. An uneven cap of fringe hung over his brow and Shane thought, for just a moment, that the orangutan must trim his own bangs. The skin covering the upper hemisphere of Nik's skull was the color of charcoal ash. His nose, unlike the promi-

This is the first photo I took of Nik. He was kind of scary at first, and I had a hard time keeping the camera from shaking. S.B.

nent noses of his chimpanzee and gorilla cousins, consisted of two dainty nostrils, slits that emerged from the top of his inner-tube-gray muzzle. The muzzle itself was about the size and shape of a fairly large grapefruit. Tufts of coarse reddish-orange hair sprouted on either side of Nik's face, and a pair of thin, rubbery lips moved independently of each other in a series of almost comical contortions.

"It's really nice to meet you," Alice offered optimistically.

"Come on, Nik, don't be shy," said Yayat. "Say hello."

Nik blinked slowly and shifted his gaze between Yayat and the children, suspiciously. Then his heavy eyelids slid slowly down over his golden-brown eyes and, keeping his eyes closed, he offered each of the children a palm-up hand. Alice and Shane looked to each other for a clue about what to do next.

"What's he doing?" whispered Shane.

"I don't know, maybe he wants to check our pulse," said Alice.

"Or our vibes," said Shane.

Tentatively, Alice laid her hand in Nik's palm and felt the heat radiating from his body. Shane laid his hand in the orangutan's other open palm. Nik seemed to go into a kind of trance for what seemed like a long time but was probably just a few seconds. Alice noticed, as her hand rested in Nik's left palm, that the tip of his index finger was missing. She wondered what kind of accident could have caused such an injury. Suddenly Nik's eyelids fluttered open and a long kissing sound escaped his lips. His upper lip stretched over his enormous yellow teeth in a wide grin. "Welcome to our forest," he said, and Shane and Alice each breathed a sigh of relief.

"Yayat and I have to be getting back to our own part of the forest now," said Siti, when she saw that Nik had accepted Alice and Shane.

"That's right," agreed Yayat. "This really isn't our neck of the woods, you know."

"You're just going to leave us here?" asked Alice, a little concerned that their gibbon guides would abandon them to an orangutan they hardly knew.

"How are we supposed to get back?" said Shane.

"Don't worry, Nik will take good care of you," Siti said.

"He'll take you to meet the Old Man," said Yayat. "Right, Nik?"

"You'll be safe with me," Nik assured them, "but I can't promise that we'll actually find the Old Man."

"That's right, you'll be safe," said Yayat. "I mean, who's going to mess with Nik?"

The gibbons scampered up a tree and moments later were swinging freely from branch to branch high in the canopy.

"Ahhh, freedom," called Yayat elatedly. "There's nothing like losing it to make you appreciate how precious it is."

"Look at them," said Shane, craning his neck and squinting into the canopy for a last glimpse of the gibbons. "I wonder what it's like to swing through the trees like that. It must feel really cool."

"Good-bye Alice, good-bye Shane, don't forget us," Siti and Yayat sang in unison. Then leaping onto a strangler fig root, they both disappeared into the camouflage of the forest.

Like all orangutans, Nik was arboreal, and spent most of his time eating and sleeping in the canopy high above the forest floor. Though his body, with its long, strong arms and short legs, was well suited for life in the trees, he was more or less at home on the ground as well. He would descend to the forest floor occasionally to drink from streams, or to dig for termites and beetle larvae in decaying logs. He would sometimes climb down when he had a yearning for sharp tasting wild ginger, the succulent heart of a forest palm, or other foods that broke the monotony of his usual fruit, leaf and bark diet.

As Nik led Alice and Shane deeper into the steamy dark woods, the foliage on the forest floor became sparse due to the lack of sunlight. Nik's body pitched slightly forward as he ambled along the path, alternately walking on his fists and on the backs of his hands. The curve of Nik's legs, which were half as long as his arms, forced him to walk duck-toed.

"Nik has the strangest walk," Alice whispered to Shane over her shoulder as they followed the orangutan through the understory.

"He walks sort of like a crab," said Shane, who was bringing up the rear. This was of course not accurate: Nik walked nothing like a crab. Yet to see him loping along with his gangly, slightly sideways gait, the animal he reminded Shane of most was a crab. Suddenly, as if in retaliation for his crab remark, Shane's San Francisco Giants cap was plucked from his head.

"Hey!" said Shane. Turning around, he saw his cap floating in mid air over the path, suspended from a long, thorny rattan tendril. "Did you see that?"

"If you can keep your hat on when everyone else is losing theirs," said Alice, paraphrasing a quote she'd once heard as she disentangled Shane's cap, "you're using too much gel."

The path eventually veered downhill and led the hikers to a marsh filled with water the color of strong tea. The water was only a foot or so deep, and leaves and branches were visible beneath the surface. The air around this swampy depression was stiflingly hot and humid; Alice's and Shane's clothing was soon soaked through with perspiration. Unwittingly, they walked into a spiraling black tornado of mosquitoes, which immediately attacked them as if they were hamburgers at a Fourth of July picnic.

"Dang," said Shane, as he ran out of the mosquito cloud. "These skeeters are bound and determined to make a meal out of me."

"What the heck is this thing?" shrieked Alice. She pulled a black, worm-like creature about an inch long from the bare skin just above her sock. A small red circle marked the spot where the organism had briefly affixed itself to her leg.

"That sucker's a leech," said Shane, with great certainty.

"Oh, yuck," said Alice, flicking the parasitical appendage into the swamp. Concentric circles spread as it vanished beneath the surface of the amber water.

"Tuck your pant legs into your socks," suggested Shane.

"Good idea," said Alice, pulling her socks up as high on her legs as they would stretch, covering her trouser cuffs.

With the mosquitoes behind them, Alice stopped to rummage through her backpack and pulled out a squeeze bottle of insect repellent, an effective deterrent in spite of its relatively low concentration of highly toxic Deet. "Spray some of this on your clothes," said Alice, passing the repellent to Shane. "It's pretty awful stuff, but it keeps the bugs away."

"I thought I had mine with me, but I guess I don't," said Shane. "When I left the house this morning I didn't figure I'd be taking a stroll through the jungle with an orangutan."

When Shane finished protecting himself against future mosquito attacks, he offered some of the repellent to Nik, who wagged his deformed finger and shook his head from side to side. "Never touch the stuff," he said.

After Alice sprayed repellent on her clothes and skin, they proceeded along the path. They crossed a wooden catwalk over the knee-deep swamp, then climbed steadily until they reached the spine of another ridge.

"This country sure has a lot of ups and downs to it," remarked Shane, out of breath and red-faced from the steep climb. "Sort of like a roller without no coaster."

"Without any coaster," corrected Alice, unable to resist.

They walked in single file along the narrow trail. The path veered downward again, away from the ridge, and the forest again grew darker and more ominous.

"Did the sun duck behind a cloud or something?" said Shane. "Getting awfully shady in here."

"Canopy's thicker in this part of the forest," said Nik. "The bigger the leaves, the less light reaches the forest floor."

"When we were studying rain forest ecology in school, we learned that only about five percent of the light actually makes it down to the forest floor," said Alice. "But what I want to know is how do they know that? How can they tell when there's only five percent of the light?"

Nik shrugged. "That's not something I really need to know."

"They probably have some sort of light meter, like what's in my camera," Shane theorized. "Maybe someone climbs up and reads the light that's above the trees and then someone else reads the light on the forest floor. Then you can subtract one reading from the other and figure a percentage from that."

"Makes sense, I guess," said Alice.

Shane picked up a curled brown leaf that had fallen on a fan-shaped coconut palm just off the trail. "Check this out, Alice," he said holding it up for her to examine. "It's thicker than shoe leather."

"That's as big as my dad's shoe," said Alice. "Yep, this is a size ten-and-a-half leaf."

Nik looked at the leaf and said, "Dipterocarp. About forty different kinds of these grow around here."

"Do you eat this kind of leaf?" Alice asked.

"Not usually," said Nik, shaking his head. "I prefer fruits when I can find them."

"Nik," said Alice, pointing to the scar on his hand, and the missing tip of his finger, "how did you hurt your finger?"

Nik stared at his finger and Alice could almost feel him peeling back the pages of his memory. "It happened a long time ago," said Nik. "This scar goes much deeper than what you see here."

"What do you mean?" asked Shane, examining Nik's scar.

"It happened during my first year, when I was taken from my mother," said Nik.

"Someone took you from your mother? Who?" said Alice incredulously. "Why would anyone want to do that?"

"Some twolegs have the idea that orangutans make good pets."

"People think parrots make good pets, too," said Alice, "but I'm not so sure they do. Wild animals don't make good pets. That's what dogs and cats are for."

"Someone took you from your mother so they could keep you as a pet?" asked Shane.

"Not exactly. They stole me so they could sell me to someone else, who would then sell me to another person who wanted a baby orangutan as a pet," said Nik, his normally smooth deep voice becoming tight with the memory. "My mother tried to protect me, but..."

"But what?" said Shane. "What the heck happened?"

"Some poachers spotted my mother and me in a tree near a village. We were minding our own business. I was clinging to her the way all baby orangutans do for the first few years of their lives, and she was showing me a new kind of fruit to eat."

"My dad told me baby orangutans stay with their mothers for about eight years," said Alice. "Is that true?"

"That's about right," said Nik. "A young orangutan stays with its mother until he learns enough to fend for himself, or until another baby is born. Could take eight years, could take six. Might even take ten. It all depends on how quickly the baby learns to survive in the forest on its own."

"The parents don't kick them out of the nest before they're ready, like humans sometimes do, huh, Nik?" said Shane.

"I couldn't say," said Nik, "but the bond between mothers and babies is very strong."

"As strong as human babies and their mothers?" asked Alice.

"At least, maybe even stronger."

"So what happened after they spotted you?" asked Alice, eager to hear the rest of Nik's story.

"Mother and I were exploring a durian tree. We weren't very high up, maybe about as high as those branches up there," said Nik, pointing to a tree just ahead of them whose lower limbs were twenty feet above the forest floor. "Unfortunately, there was another tree growing right next to the durian. There were two men—I remember their faces as clearly as if it happened yesterday. They wore dirty shirts and ragged shorts, and rubber sandals that slapped the bottom of their feet when they walked. I can still hear that slap, slap, slap as they walked through the forest. And they both carried machetes."

"Oh geez," said Alice.

"One of the men shinnied up the tree next to the one we were in. The machete was stuck in his belt and hung down behind him. He inched his way up the tree, closer and closer, but my mother didn't move."

"Didn't she try to get away?" asked Shane.

"I think she may have been too afraid to move," said Nik. "Anyway, the man in the tree was holding on with his legs and one arm and reaching out with the other, trying to pull me off my mother, but I was holding on as tight as I could and he couldn't pull me off. Mother lunged for the man's arm and bit him. He screamed and the whole forest echoed with the sound, but his wound was not that serious. Still, he was angry, very, very angry. He reached behind his back and pulled the machete from his belt. He held it over his head and swung it with all his might at my mother's neck."

"Oh no," said Alice, burying her face in her hands.

"I think I'm going to be sick," said Shane.

"With one slash of the blade, my mother's head was… gone. And the tip of my finger was gone, too."

"Oh Nik, that's the most horrible thing I've ever heard," said Alice.

"Sickening," said Shane. "That's what it is."

"Horrible, sickening. Yes, it was both of those and more. But it happens all the time. The only way a poacher can get a baby is to kill its mother," said Nik. "I still remember holding on to Mother's body and watching her head tumbling over and over as it fell, her eyes wide open, an expression of terror still on her beautiful face. And I'll never forget the sound her head made when it hit the forest floor and the way it bounced and rolled down the hill through the dry leaves and finally splashed into the swamp."

"Oh my God," said Alice.

Shane, gazing at Nik, was unable to speak.

"But what happened to you?" asked Alice, after a short silence. "You must have fallen out of the tree, too."

"Yes, of course," said Nik. "Mother's body clung to the tree trunk for what seemed like a long time and then it just sort of relaxed and fell away with me still holding on. I landed on top of her soft body, so in that way she succeeded in saving my life after all."

"Aw, man," said Shane, shaking his head.

"The second man ran down the hill and waded into the swamp to fetch my mother's head, which was bobbing in the water. He tossed her head in a plastic basket and threw me in there, too. I was so afraid. I wrapped my arms around my mother's head and hung on as tightly as I could as the two of them hurried back to the village, laughing and slapping hands and jabbering on about all the money they would make when they sold me to the black-market traders."

"You've got to be kidding, right?" said Shane, though he knew Nik was not kidding.

"No, Shane, I am quite serious," said Nik solemnly. "There is no limit to the cruelty your species is capable of inflicting on the other inhabitants of this planet. No limit at all."

"There's no limit to the cruelty we inflict on each other, either," said Alice.

"But I thought they wanted you," said Shane. "Why would they want... you know... your mother's head?"

"An orangutan skull is a popular souvenir for tourists. Sometimes a villager carves a design into the bone after the flesh has been scraped off. Sometimes they rub ashes into the design, or burn it, to make it look old. Sometimes they just boil the skull until the brain dissolves and the flesh falls off, and sell it just like that. Tourists find a skull in a market or a shop and think they have discovered a rare artifact of some kind. They see the carving and think it has some sort of religious significance—they think it means something. They don't stop to think that what it really means is that the head they are buying belonged to someone else and that someone has been killed so they can have their precious souvenir to put on their shelf back home. It doesn't even occur to them to ask where the skull came from."

"Geez, you'd think it'd be illegal to sell skulls from an endangered species like orangutans," said Alice.

"It is illegal, but what good is a law that is not enforced?" said Nik. "If the shop owner does get caught selling an orangutan skull, or a gall bladder or claws from a sun bear, or plumes from a hornbill, he just pays a fine and is back in business the same day, sending the poachers out for more skulls and plumes and bear claws. There are plenty of people willing to kill animals for no other reason than to steal their babies and take their heads and body parts. And there is no shortage of empty-headed tourists to buy them."

"Seems like the real criminals in this business are the ignorant tourists who create the demand for this stuff in the first place," said Alice.

"Yes," said Nik, "the tourists, and the people who think they want an orangutan for a pet."

"What happened to you when the men took you to the village?" said Shane.

Nik ran his long fingers over his skull and sighed. "Oh, I don't know if I want to get into that," he said. "At least not right now."

CHAPTER 6

Hey, Jude

T he trio of primates plodded through the rain forest in silence, moving slowly to conserve the energy that was so easily drained by the tropical heat. As they walked, the incessant buzzing of unseen cicadas assaulted their ears. They heard the urgent chatter of proboscis monkeys squabbling over some chewy morsel in the trees. Then the path forked. One path, slick ochre mud textured with the footprints and indentations of a thousand small stampedes, led upward toward the ridge and higher ground. The other fork, vague with disuse, spiraled down into a forested valley where a cathedral of towering hardwoods competed for the sun's light like basketball players jumping for a rebound. Nik scratched under his arm while he considered the two choices before them. "Decision time," he said. "The right path is the ridge trail, and the one most forest dwellers use."

"What about the left one?" asked Shane.

"That one is much less traveled and leads down to a stream," said Nik. "Which one do you want to take?"

"Shoot, I don't know," said Shane. "You're the guide."

"I don't know, either," said Alice wiping the sweat from her brow.

"Maybe we should stick with the ridge trail like the rest of the animals," said Shane.

"That'd be safe," agreed Nik.

"We could take the other one," said Alice. "It'd be more of an adventure."

"There's no chance we'll get lost, is there?" asked Shane worriedly.

"Lost?" said Nik, his rubbery lips folding back over his yellow teeth so that it looked as if he'd swallowed an entire piano. "What do you mean?"

"What about the Old Man of the Forest?" said Alice. "Which trail would lead us to him?"

"Maybe both," said Nik. "But then again, maybe neither. We won't find the Old Man, he'll find us."

"Okay, then I say we go with the one less traveled," said Alice, looking to Shane for consensus. "I mean, how many times are we going to be in Borneo, right? We might as well make the most of it."

"What do you think, Shane?" said Nik.

"Yeah, Alice is right, we're only going to be here once. I guess we should take the low road," said Shane, with a shrug. "And besides, it's downhill."

"But it's uphill on the way back," said Alice.

The less-traveled trail was steep and its many slick, muddy switchbacks made navigation difficult. They walked carefully, eyes to the ground, until their progress was arrested by a narrow ravine with a miniature forest of feathery ferns guarding the bank on either side. Fast-moving white water tumbled through the narrow gorge on its way to a tributary on the valley floor.

"Oh man, how're we gonna get over that?" asked Shane, though the gap was only five feet wide, easy jumping distance for a good jumper. "Maybe we should've taken the ridge trail."

"Give me your backpack," said Alice.

"Why?" said Shane, wiggling out of the shoulder straps nonetheless.

Alice threw Shane's backpack and then her own over the cascading water. The packs landed with soft thuds and were swallowed up by the ferns.

"Hey! Why'd you do that?"

"Now it's just a matter of how we're going to get over the creek, not if."

"Dang, girl! All my stuff's in there—my toilet paper and everything!"

"All the more reason to get across."

Nik could move through the forest terrestrially or arboreally with equal ease so the rushing stream was no problem to him. For a being of his considerable skills, there were many ways to cross a stream, and he couldn't understand why Alice and Shane were making such a large issue of such a small obstacle. It would be up to him to show the way. So Nik walked up a slender bintawa tree whose trunk was no thicker than his neck. When the tree started to bend under his weight, he climbed a bit higher and began to rock back and forth so that from a distance he looked like a hairy red weight on a giant forest metronome. When the swaying tree's arc carried him over the rushing stream, he simply hung by his hands and dropped into the bed of ferns on the other side.

"You know Nik, no one likes a showoff," said Shane, smiling. "All right, stand back and let me do my thing."

"Your thing?" said Alice.

Shane backtracked about thirty feet up the trail and said, "Okay, here goes." And with that he ran as fast as he could. When he reached the edge of the slippery bank he leaped, and if it hadn't been for a creeping vine that crossed the trail like an untied shoelace, he would have made it. Panicking, he grabbed a root that was protruding from the bank on the other side and held on, but his legs dangled down the muddy bank and his shoes could find no purchase. Nik, who had been watching with the kind of detached amusement that only orangutans are capable of, grabbed Shane by the forearms and pulled him to safety as if he weighed nothing at all.

"Thanks, Nik," said Shane, his face flushed with embarrassment. "I guess I underestimated the distance."

"Or overestimated your jumping ability," said Alice with a grin.

Alice decided not to follow Shane's lead. If he couldn't make it, she doubted that she could. She spotted a liana, a vine dangling down from the canopy like a garden hose full of kinks, on the far side of the ravine. She picked up a broken branch with a hook at one end, perhaps the remnant of an orangutan nest, and pulled off its small, leafy twigs. Using the branch, she hooked the vine and pulled it toward her until it was close enough for her to grab.

"Ah, tools," said Nik from his and Shane's side of the bank.

Holding the liana in one hand, Alice retreated up the hill and climbed onto a log that laid parallel with the steep slope. She stood with the liana in both hands like a Tarzan—or, in her case, a Tarzana—for the new millennium. She tugged on the vine to test its strength, drew a deep breath and said, "Okay, here goes." She ran a few feet down the log and then leaped, free falling until the slack in the vine was taken up. With a pulpy snap that rustled the leaves high in the canopy, the vine straightened and carried her over the gorge. She cleared the ravine easily and dropped into the ferns on the other side.

Alice laughed, giddy with triumph. "My dad will be glad to know all those rock-climbing and gymnastic lessons finally came in handy."

A few minutes later they were picking their way through an area of the forest where nibung palms grew. Stiff needles stood out from the nibung trunks like sharp bayonets, ready to rip and tear the skin of any unwary predators. Alice and Shane ducked beneath serdang leaves, arrays of sword-like fronds as big around as truck tires. They wiggled over decaying logs that were as high as overstuffed chairs and that crumbled to the consistency of potting soil when touched. Nearly every tree or sapling was wrapped with a vine, which depended on the host tree's strength and vertical structure to transport it up to the sun. And in this lush part of the forest epiphytes—staghorn ferns or delicate orchids—clung to almost every branch fork, leaching nutrients from their host trees. In contrast to drier parts of the rain forest, the atmosphere in the damp glade was thick and pungent with the invigorating aroma of rot and decay. Here, life emerged from death. Where a giant tree once had stood, a shaft of sunlight penetrated the canopy. In the cone of transparent, buttery light a flock of butterflies, the tops of their wings as shiny as newly minted pennies and the undersides as silvery as aluminum foil, swirled in a spiraling vortex, like gum wrappers in a blender.

"Look at that, they're winking on and off like strobe lights," said Shane when he saw the dancing butterflies. "Dang, that's awesome!"

Farther along the trail they came upon a small cabin with boarded-up windows. A sign nailed to it read, "Camp Sinaga."

"What the heck is this place?" said Shane, tossing his backpack onto a wooden table on the cabin porch. As mosquitoes whined around his ears he rifled through his pack for his water bottle and guzzled deeply. "I mean, who'd build a cabin way the heck out here in the middle of a Borneo rain forest?"

"Does someone live here, Nik?" asked Alice.

"Not at the moment," said Nik. "This is a former release station."

"Release station?"

"Orangutans that have been orphaned—as I was—or been confiscated from poachers or surrendered by their so-called owners, sometimes end up in a rehabilitation center. At least, the lucky ones do. In the rehab center they are given food and shelter and taught the skills they will need to survive once they are released back into the forest. Sometimes they stay at the rehab center for several years."

"Wow," said Alice, "that's a long time."

"For orphaned orangutans, survival is something that must be learned. If we're going to make it on our own, we need to learn what foods are available in the forest and how to find them."

"You mean orangutans have to be taught what to eat?" asked Shane. "Don't they, you know, already know that stuff?"

"Yeah," said Alice. "Don't they have a food instinct or something?"

"Were you born knowing what to eat?" Nik asked Shane.

"Well, shoot, I guess I never gave it much thought," said Shane. "But now that you mention it, it seems like I didn't discover Pringles until I was about six or so."

"Pringles? What is Pringles?"

"It's a weird kind of potato chip," said Alice. "They take a potato and grind it up and then put it back together again and make this potato chip thing out of it."

"That seems like a lot of trouble to go through with something that's ready to eat when you pull it out of the ground," said Nik. "How did you first learn about these Pringle things, Shane?"

"A kid at school had some in his lunch and I traded some marbles for them."

"Well, anyway," said Nik, "an orangutan has to learn what to eat just as you did. Usually, the mothers teach the babies how to find food in the forest. But unfortunately, orphans don't have mothers to teach them, so the job falls to the twolegs who work in the rehab center."

"Wouldn't that be a hard thing for a twoleg to teach an orangutan?" asked Alice.

"It is very difficult," said Nik. "The ultimate test of how well the orphans have learned is whether they survive in the forest once they are on their own. Until the orphans are making independent choices, the twolegs don't know for sure whether they have acquired enough skills to survive independently. So they build camps like this one where twolegs can live and work while they monitor how the released orangutans are doing on their own."

"Is this where you were released, Nik?" asked Alice.

"Yes," said Nik, "I've been living on my own for three years now, but I am one of the success stories. There are plenty of failures, as well."

Just then they heard a deep rattling cough. A timid voice from the canopy squeaked, "Nikki, is that you?"

Nik looked up to see a small female orangutan hanging by one long arm from a branch high above the forest floor. "Hey, Jude," Nik called, shading his eyes with a raft of long fingers. "It's been a while…how're you doing?"

"Who are those twolegs with you, Nikki? I don't recognize them," Jude answered, her squeaky voice weak and worried.

"It's okay, they're harmless. Come down and say hello."

"You sure, Nikki, you sure?"

Nik turned to Alice and Shane and whispered, "Jude's very shy. She's had kind of a tough life, which has left her very suspicious of twolegs." Nik looked up at Jude and said, "It's safe, they're friends. Come on down."

Jude wrapped her bony fingers around the tree trunk and backed down slowly. When she reached the forest floor she climbed onto a fallen log and squatted in a patch of sunlight at its far end, drawing her legs to her thin chest and folding her arms around them so that she resembled a hairy Easter egg. She cast a shy glance at Shane and Alice out of the corner of her eye and waited indifferently, as if she were waiting for a bus that might or might not come.

When Nik ambled over and sat next to Jude, he did not like what he saw. Jude's skin hung loosely on her slight frame. Her kneecaps protruded like knobs from her thin legs. What remained of her hair was wispy and dull, in sharp contrast to Nik's coarse but shiny locks. Her shoulder blades were skin-covered ridges that stood out from her back like sails. She had about her the ghostly look of the malnourished.

"How have you been, my friend?" asked Nik, settling beside her on the log.

"Oh, you know, Nikki, some days are filled with fruit and termites and others… are not," said Jude.

"Yes, I know what you mean," said Nik. "These are my friends, Alice and Shane."

Jude stared at the teenagers and emitted a small kiss-squeak.

"Howdy," said Shane.

"Hey, Jude," said Alice.

"Are you having trouble finding enough to eat, Jude?" Nik asked his friend.

"The drought and the fires have been tough on all of us forest dwellers," said Jude. "There's a lot of competition for what little fruit there is. The bats have taken most of it. Mostly I've been eating rattan down by the river, where things are still green. Last night I broke into the cabin and stole some noodles. I'm not proud of it, but an orangutan's got to do what she's got to do."

"Desperate times call for desperate measures," said Nik, scratching his back. "How're your lungs?"

"Oh, they're better, I guess," said Jude, suddenly convulsing with a coughing fit. "I'm not so short of breath all the time, like I used to be, but today I'm not so good."

Nik turned to Alice and Shane, who were now seated next to him on the log, and explained, "Jude was raised by a military man who taught her to drink martinis and smoke cigarettes. When she came to the rehab center she was in pretty bad shape."

"He taught her to drink and smoke?" said Shane. "That don't make a lick of sense."

"Doesn't," said Alice. "Doesn't make a lick of sense."

"Well, it don't, does it?" said Shane, smiling slyly at Alice to let her know he didn't care for her correcting his grammar. Shaking his head, Shane continued, "Why the heck would anyone give an orangutan cigarettes and booze?"

"That's not all they gave her," said Nik. "When she came to the center she had tuberculosis, too."

"Orangutans can get TB?" said Alice. "I didn't know that."

"And hepatitis, too," Jude chimed in weakly.

"Jude's one of the lucky ones," said Nik, though you could tell by the tone of his voice he didn't believe that Jude was all that lucky. "Ever heard of an orangutan named Romeo?" Alice and Shane shook their heads. "He's kind of famous, for an orangutan. He was one of the Taiwan Ten, a bunch of poached babies who were confiscated at the Taiwan airport a few years ago. They were all sent back to Borneo and put into rehab. The poor guy picked up tuberculosis somewhere along the way and every time they think they've got him cured, he tests positive again."

"Why does he test positive if he's cured?" said Alice.

"He just can't seem to shake it completely."

"So, what does that mean for Romeo?"

"It means Romeo is chronic, and that means he will never be released into the wilderness where he might come into contact with other orangutans that he might possibly infect. He is doomed to live forever in a cage in the rehab center. Oh, he'll be cared for as long as the rehab center stays in business, but he'll never know what it's like to eat wild figs, or build a nest high in the canopy and wake up before dawn to the call of gibbons."

"Those gibbons get up way too early to suit me," said Jude.

"Count your blessings, Jude," said Nik. "You could be waking up every morning to the roar of buses and motorbikes."

"I know, Nikki, but sometimes I think it'd be better if I never left rehab. Life is so hard for me out here."

"I know it is, Jude," said Nik. "But every day it gets a little easier, trust me."

"You kids wouldn't have any crackers you could spare, would you?" said Jude. "Or maybe some Gummi Bears?"

Shane dug into his backpack. "Hey, here's a pack of Oreos, you want them?"

"You're too kind."

"Hey, here's some peanuts from the airplane," said Alice, perplexed. "That's funny. I don't remember putting them in my backpack."

"I didn't pack any Oreos, either," said Shane.

"No Gummi Bears?" said Jude disappointedly.

"Sorry," said Alice and Shane in unison.

"I don't miss the Marlboros and the martinis, but I do miss the Gummi Bears."

"I haven't had a Gummi Bear since my braces went on," said Alice.

"Hey Jude," said Shane, "how'd you end up with the military man, anyway?"

"Oh," sighed Jude, "in the usual way."

"The usual way?" said Alice. "What do you mean?"

"My mother and I were living in a forest on the outskirts of town. Of course our forest wasn't always on the outskirts of town, it used to be wilderness. But the town kept getting closer and closer. Little farms started springing up. Twolegs started clearing the forest and planting gardens and banana orchards, and our big forest kept getting smaller and smaller as the twolegs cut down the fruit trees that gave us food and the tall trees that gave us shelter."

"Hmmm," mused Alice. "Clearing the land for agriculture—I saw it from the airplane."

"All I know is that pretty soon, our whole forest was surrounded by little farms and we were living on this island of trees right in the middle of it. The birds could just fly someplace else, but we were stuck. Food was hard to find because more of us were competing for less and less food. Everything was out of balance. One day my mother decided to sneak into a banana plantation on the edge of our forest to pick a few bananas. We didn't think anyone would mind."

"Uh-oh," said Shane.

"You asked," said Alice with a frown.

"My mother was picking bananas and handing them to me and I was eating them as fast as I could because I was so hungry. Then I heard an explosion and saw my mother crumple to the ground. She was bleeding from a hole in her chest. She twitched a couple of times and groaned, and then she was still. A man came running toward us across a field. I pulled on my mother's arm. When she didn't get up I started screaming and jumping up and down. The man had a net and he threw it over me and I got all tangled up in it and couldn't move and the man kept wrapping more and more net around me until I was like a fly in a spider's web. I was just two years old."

"What'd they do with you?" asked Alice.

"They put me in a little crate and took me into town, and sold me at the night market."

"To the military man?" said Shane.

"Yes, to the military man."

"So, how did you get from the military man to the rehabilitation center?" asked Alice.

"There was an article in the paper saying that if you owned an orangutan and wanted to give it up, you wouldn't be prosecuted."

"So, owning an orangutan is against the law?" said Shane.

"Yes, it is," said Nik. "But that doesn't stop anyone. The police just look the other way."

"But my owner's wife never liked me. I guess I wasn't enough like a child. She always wanted to have a child of her own, but she just couldn't. She used to beat me when I soiled my diaper or threw her folded laundry around the room. So when the article appeared, the military man just took me down to the rehabilitation center and turned me over."

"And how long were you there?" asked Alice.

"Three years," said Jude.

Nik looked at the sun edging closer to the tops of the trees and said, "We'd better be getting down the trail, kids. We've still got a long hike in front of us."

"Where are you headed, Nikki?"

"I'm taking them to meet the Old Man," said Nik.

"Do you know him, Jude?" asked Shane.

"No," said Jude, "but I've heard his call."

That evening toward dusk, when the bats were darting through the peach-colored sky like broken birds, consuming mouthful upon mouthful of mosquitoes and other flying insects, Jude climbed an ulin tree. The ulin was close to an abundantly fruiting fig that would provide her with a succulent breakfast in the morning. It was so close that a few of its figgy tendrils had invaded the crown of the ulin. Though Jude was a young orangutan whose childbearing years were ahead of her, she knew better than to build her nest in a fruit-bearing tree, where she, and her baby if she ever had a baby, would be vulnerable to the nocturnal civets and clouded leopards who prowled fruit trees in search of chewy treats like fruit bats and mice. A clouded leopard or civet would enjoy nothing better than a tender morsel such as baby orangutan.

Jude built her nest and gave it a comfort test. Needs a little more padding to protect these bones, she thought. Venturing out on a limb to pick a handful of ulin leaves, she spotted a solitary orange fig, the lone survivor of what had been an entire cluster. That fig, thought Jude, would make a perfect snack before she climbed into her nest for the evening. It wasn't a Gummi Bear, but it was sweet and chewy. She reached out her long arms, but the fig dangled just beyond her extended fingers. Scooting a little farther out on the ulin branch, she tried again. She stretched her thin arm as far as she could, but the fig was still just beyond her outstretched fingers. Again she scooted forward, and the ulin branch began to give. Then, suddenly, perhaps because the drought had made it brittle, the

I took this photo of Jude just after I told her we didn't have any Gummi Bears. She was kind of bummed. S.B.

branch snapped. Down, down through twilight Jude tumbled, bouncing from branch to branch until she hit the forest floor with a sickening thud. Even more frightening than the thud was a duet of sharp cracks that accompanied her fall.

On the forest floor, Jude writhed in pain. She struggled up to sit on her haunches and held her throbbing arm. Something was terribly wrong: There was a joint in her arm where one had not been before. Her hand and wrist and some of her arm dangled straight down where her brittle bones had snapped. She tried to stand and realized then that something was wrong with her leg, too. She lay back and tried to think what she would do next. If only she could get back to her nest, she thought, maybe she would be all right in the morning. She must get up to her nest somehow; she shouldn't spend the night unprotected on the forest floor. In great pain, she dragged herself through the leafy understory to the base of the ulin tree and looked up at the tree towering over her. The dark tangle of her nest looked far away in the top of the tree. She reached up with one arm and tried to climb, but her other arm hung uselessly at her side and would

What the Orangutan Told Alice

not obey her body's commands. She tried to stand, but her ankle buckled painfully under her weight and she cried out in pain. So as darkness fell, Jude dragged herself farther into the forest, down into the gully, down where she knew she would find cool water to quench her fiery thirst. And it was there, as she lay in the soothing mud by the slow-moving yellow water, that the clouded leopard found her.

CHAPTER 7

Termite Take-out

Termite

Nik crabbed along the path on his fists, stopping frequently to eat the succulent rattan shoots that grew along the edge of the trail. Watching Nik pull and eat the tender shoots reminded Shane of summers back home, when he and his friends pulled wheat grass shoots from the golden California fields that surrounded his house. The squeak of the rattan as it separated from the stalk was the same clean sound that wheat grass made. He remembered the sweet, tender taste of the new shoots. Watching Nik nibble reminded Shane that it had been some time since he had eaten.

"Those pretty good, Nik?" Shane called, over Alice's head.

"They are. Here, try one," said Nik, extracting two shoots and handing one to Shane and the other to Alice.

"Hmmm, tasty," said Shane.

"I like the squeaky noise they make when you pull them out," said Alice, helping herself to another.

"Rattan is one of my favorite snacks," said Nik, squatting beside a foot-tall rattan, whose leaves, normally as pointed as paring-knife blades, were blunt, as if they had been trimmed with scissors. "Look, see these leaves? This is what happens to the new leaves that are growing behind the shoot when its tip is pulled out. It's also a sure sign that there are orangutans around."

"The Old Man?" said Alice.

"Perhaps," said Nik with a shrug of his rounded shoulders.

Now that Nik had pointed them out, Alice and Shane noticed rattans everywhere, and most of them showed evidence of orangutan browsing.

"Sure seems like a lot of orangutans have been through here," said Alice. "Do you guys always use these trails?"

"Most of the time, when we're on the ground," said Nik. "We're a lot like twolegs—we take the path of least resistance when we walk through the forest."

"What other sorts of stuff do you guys eat?" Shane asked, his question prompted by the rumble in his stomach.

Nik's lips stretched tightly over his teeth into an amusing grin. "How much time do you have?"

"Time? I don't know," shrugged Shane. "You tell me."

Alice tapped the crystal of her watch, which had now fogged over. Its hands were still pointing to twelve, midnight or noon, depending on your point of view. "This stupid watch is only right twice a day."

"Well, we eat about four hundred different kinds of food," said Nik. "Mostly fruit, leaves and bark, but we eat termites, and honey, too, when we can find it. Probably the best way for you to learn what we eat is for me to treat you to lunch," said Nik as he turned off the trail and into the forest. "Follow me."

"Well, okay," said Alice apprehensively. "But I'll pass on the termites and bugs and stuff."

"I think I can probably live without termites, too," said Shane. "I'm not really all that hungry. That shoot back there kind of filled me up."

"But your stomach's growling," said Alice.

"Yeah, well, you know, that's just something it does sometimes," replied Shane.

Nik smacked his lips and said, "You're not going to try termites? Why not? You might like them."

"No way," said Shane, "they're bugs and I don't eat bugs. I don't even like to look at bugs. They bug me."

"You eat eggs, don't you, Shane?" said Nik.

"Well, sure, but so what? Eggs are different."

"Different from what?"

"From termites."

"If you can eat the embryo of a chicken, what's stopping you from eating a termite, or its larvae?"

Shane took his cap off and scratched his head. "Shoot, I never thought of it quite like that."

"It's a cultural barrier, I guess," said Alice.

"Yeah," concurred Shane, "what she said."

Nik squatted near the decaying corpse of a huge fallen tree that, with the help of termites and fungus, was slowly returning to the earth. Decomposing day by day, year by year, decade by decade, changing form, it was releasing nutrients into the soil that would nurture new generations of forest life. "Hey, we're in luck—there's a termite nest right here."

Alice and Shane squatted next to the nest. It looked like a smooth, hard blob of dried mud and was the size and shape of a double-ended goat's udder.

"Looks like one of them foam rubber Smurf footballs," observed Shane, poking the nest with a stick.

"No, no, no, like this," said Nik, wrapping his long fingers around the nest and effortlessly breaking it into equal halves. He shook the mature white termites and their larvae onto the hair near his elbow; they looked like muscle-bound grains of rice. Nik picked the wiggling morsels trapped and tangled in his coarse hair off his arm one by one. "Mmm, a particularly tasty colony," said Nik, offering the broken nest to Alice. "Change your mind?"

"Naw, they'd get stuck in my braces," said Alice sheepishly. "I don't think termites were on the list of food my orthodontist said I could eat. In fact, I think I remember her distinctly telling me not to eat termites."

"How about you, Shane? You're not wearing braces. Care to expand your culinary horizons?"

Shane looked at Alice and then to Nik, mulling over whether or not to sample a termite.

"Oh, go ahead," said Alice with a grin. "I'd try one if I wasn't wearing these darn braces."

Shane picked a plump larva out of the nest with his thumb and index finger and, after a brief hesitation, popped it into his mouth. He chewed once, then gulped it down without expression.

"Well?" said Alice, watching Shane expectantly. "What's it taste like?"

"It's hard to describe," said Shane, mimicking Nik with a smack of his lips. "I reckon you're just going to have to try one to find out. Come on, Alice. I won't tell your orthodontist. Your secret is safe with me."

"Shane!"

"Well, there's not much to them, really," said Shane, tossing two more wiggling larvae into his mouth as if they were pieces of popcorn. "They're sort of, I don't know, creamy, like... eggnog. I'd say they taste a little like... well, chicken yogurt, actually. Could you please pass the water bottle?"

"Chicken yogurt?" said Alice.

"Curiosity is a good thing," said Nik, nodding his head approvingly. "Maybe you will grow up to be a research scientist."

Alice laughed. "I hope so because I don't think you have much future as a chef."

Nik stripped a piece of bark from a strangler fig whose many roots wrapped a huge dipterocarp like a tangle of giant boa constrictors. "Care to nibble on this, Alice? Bark is another of our favorite foods."

"Uh, yeah, sure... bark I can handle," said Alice.

"Anyone can eat bark," said Shane. "It takes a real man to eat a termite."

"Or an orangutan," said Nik. "Or a sun bear."

"Oh give up, Shane," said Alice, baring her lips over her braces and managing a small bite from the bark Nik offered her.

"What's the verdict?" asked Shane.

"It tastes kind of... green," said Alice, chewing the bark thoughtfully.

"Green?" said Shane. "That's a color, not a taste."

"It's juicy, and a little bitter. Not bad, really, if this was, you know, all you had to eat."

A soft shadow flickered over them. They looked up to see two gray butterflies the size of paper towels floating like ash through the forest understory. The giant insects flapped their wings in unison and then glided in slow motion through the damp aromatic atmosphere. Their flight was so slow and effortless that the black spots on their wings were clearly visible as they floated along.

"Wow," said Shane. "Look at those butterflies! I've never seen butterflies that big."

"I feel like I'm dreaming all this," said Alice thoughtfully, as she watched the butterflies blend with the dappled light.

"Shhhhhh," said Nik suddenly, holding a huge finger to his lips and rolling his eyes. "I hear something."

Alice and Shane stopped talking and tuned their ears to the mosaic of forest sounds. They heard the *wah-wah-wah* of insects that reminded Alice of the wail made by London ambulances. There was the usual mechanical, electric buzz of cicadas in full surround sound, and the four-note monotone of Asian cuckoos somewhere in their nests. A pair of gibbons sang in the distant canopy. Dozens of other chirps, tweets, chattering calls, whines and whistles of insects, birds, frogs and squirrels provided the never-ending soundtrack to the rain forest. But other than those sounds Alice and Shane could detect nothing out of place in this deep and enchanted forest.

"What do you hear, Nik?" asked Shane.

"The sound of a pencil scratching paper," said Nik, squinting as if he were hearing with his eyes. "And the click of a shutter and the turning of a mind in a skull." Nik grinned. "It's Ibu Anne. She's in the forest."

CHAPTER 8

Ibu Anne

Pardon the intrusion, but before we go on, I'd like to tell you a little about this woman Ibu Anne, whose path Nik, Alice and Shane have crossed on their journey to meet the Old Man of the Forest. —Alice's dad

From the moment she saw her first orangutan in the rain forest of West Kalimantan in 1987, Ibu Anne—as she is respectfully known in the Indonesian community where she has lived and worked for many summers now—knew her life's work would be to interact with "the people of the forest" who inhabit the Malay Archipelago islands of Borneo and Sumatra.

I met Anne when she and Balikpapan Orangutan Society co-chair Christine Luckett picked me up at the Balikpapan airport on my first journey to Borneo in May 1998. The first thing I noticed about Anne was her open, easy smile and the extraordinarily confused tangle of auburn curls that surrounded her small, heart-shaped face. Anne later admitted that this was an artificially created tangle, not a natural one, and the only hairstyle that suited her life in the bush. If you look closely, you'll see that some wiry strands of silver have crept into her voluminous hairscape now that she's turned the corner on fifty. Sitting across a

Ibu Anne.

table from her for the first time, I imagined the frog-collecting, green-eyed, freckle-faced girl in blazing red pigtails that she must have been growing up on the Saskatchewan prairie.

Curled locks are all that is artificial about this thoroughly practical woman. Anne understands her environment and dresses accordingly. In the rain forest and around the Wanariset Orangutan Reintroduction Center, she wears long-sleeved shirts of thick cotton that she buys at the mall in Balikpapan for three dollars each. (Malls? In Borneo? Yes, I'm afraid so.) Her pants, also constructed of thick cotton, are likewise purchased at Indonesia's bargain prices. A woman with Anne's rain forest experience is not the target market for the latest light-weight, stick-to-your-skin, miracle-fabric shirts with their flow-through vents that allow mosquitoes and leeches access to your body. When Anne is in the forest, she wears knee-high rubber boots with knobby soles, or ordinary ankle-height hiking boots, often pulled over canvas "leech stockings" which are cinched just below the knee. "What's the point of wearing Gore-tex," she said to me once, "when you're wading through a swamp that's up to your knees?"

Anne's practical nature extends to transportation as well. There are several ways to get from downtown Balikpapan to the orangutan rehabilitation center, 38 km away along the Balikpapan-Samarinda highway. A driver from an expensive (by Indonesian standards) hotel will be happy to drive you for 100,000 rupiah, or about fourteen U.S. dollars. Or, you can hail your own private cab to take you to your destination for 50,000 rupiah. Or, you can take a taxi to the bus station and then a bus to Wanariset for a combined total of fifty cents. "You can pay more if you want to," says Anne, with her nose stuck in the *Jakarta Post*, "but what's the point?"

Nor is she easily impressed. If you tell Anne you want to see orangutans, she'll direct you to the nearest zoo. If you tell her you are interested in seeing orangutans in Borneo, you'd better have a good reason; "because I want to," won't be good enough. Anne knows her *Homo sapien* kin have pushed orangutans to their precarious perch overlooking the dark chasm of extinction. As far as Anne is concerned, too many humans inhabit the earth, and not enough orangutans.

Through the course of my multi-careered life, I've worked with many people, some successful, some not. The unsuccessful ones, those who attained a certain level of comfort or education and then stopped growing, saw no reason to work any harder than was minimally necessary. And that's okay; not everybody can carry the ball on every play. But the people I know who are truly successful (and by this I do not mean financially successful but rather those who have realized their dreams), share two common characteristics: they are focused, and they work hard. Without a doubt, Ibu Anne is the most focused individual and the hardest worker I have met or expect to meet during the course of my lifetime.

So now that I've told you who she is, let's look at what she is. We live in a world that likes to define people with titles. In the academic world in which Anne lives nine months of the year, she is known as a "primate psychologist." Now, let's take a survey: raise your hand if you know a primate psychologist. Hmmm, no hands. One of the reasons for that is that there just aren't very many people engaged in the kind of work to which Ibu Anne has dedicated her life. When I asked Anne what it was, exactly, that fascinated her about orangutans, she told me, "I want to learn how they think." Consider that statement a moment. Many people, scientists and laymen alike, question whether animals think at all. But to Ibu Anne, it's a foregone conclusion. She already knows that orangutans think. She has proved it, to herself and to the academic community, through years of observations and scientific research. Now she spends months at a time in the forest, camping out with the monitor lizards and the screaming cicadas. There, each day, Ibu Anne and her Indonesian assistants rise before dawn to wade through leech-infested peat swamps and tangles of thorny vegetation. Their eyes scan the canopy, their fingers hold pencils that record their observations in notebooks as they follow the elusive and mysterious orangutan, hoping for clues that will bring them closer to learning how and what these creatures think.

Anne probably knows as much about rehabilitant orangutans as any person on earth. She knows how they live, what they eat, and how they interact with each other. She knows that they are individuals as different from each other as you are from Alice and Shane. She knows that they are in big trouble and she knows why. Anne is a woman with strong opinions and she is not afraid to express them, even though what she has to say may not always be what people want to hear. So when she speaks to you from the pages of this book, I hope you'll listen carefully. Like the orangutans and Borneo itself, she has much to teach us.

Well, enough proselytizing from me. Looks as if Anne's invited Alice and Shane to stay for dinner and spend the night. Let's pull this leaf aside and take a peek at what's cooking.

CHAPTER 9

Alice and Shane's Dinner with Anne

S hane and Alice plodded along after Anne on the trail that led to Camp Djamaludin, the rustic research outpost where Anne sometimes lived when she studied orangutans in their natural habitat. A few notes, plucked from a guitar, floated through the trees. "Listen," said Alice. "Do you hear that? Someone's playing a guitar."

"That's Iyan," Anne called over her shoulder. "We're almost to camp."

"Who's Iyan?" asked Alice.

"He's a forest technician who has been helping me count orangutan nests," said Anne. "He's a very bright young man with a talent for botany. He can tell you the vernacular and Latin names of most all of the plants orangutans eat in the forest."

The guitar melody defined itself as they neared the camp, and Alice cocked her head in recognition of the clear notes wafting through the trees. "That's 'Let It Be,'" said Alice, and the thought occurred to her that this song was a perfect accompaniment for a trek through this sanctuary forest.

"Yes, I think you're right," said Anne as she pulled aside a thorny stalk to allow Alice and Shane to pass. "Aren't you a little young to know the music of the Beatles?"

"My dad plays their music all the time," said Alice. "The Beatles, Bob Dylan and Leonard Cohen, over and over and over again. Those are his favorites."

"Maybe Iyan knows some country and western tunes," said Shane hopefully. "Garth, McGraw. A little Merle would be awesome."

Later that evening a cool breeze dissipated the heat of the day as Alice and Shane relaxed on the deck at Camp Djamaludin. In the distance they could hear the cracking of branches as an orangutan prepared its evening nest. Alice and Shane sat across from Anne and Iyan at the picnic table that served as desk, lab bench, and dinner table. A kerosene lamp burned beside the steaming bowl of noodles and rice that Iyan had prepared. Above the table, a pair of small bats scoured the damp air for mosquitoes. The forest sighed, leaves rustled in the canopy, and the lamplight flickered, its yellow-orange flame dancing in Anne's glasses.

"So, tell me, how is it that you two happen to find yourselves in Borneo?" Anne asked Shane and Alice.

"I came with my dad," said Alice. "He's working on a book about orangutans and he's here to do some research."

"A book about orangutans?" said Anne. "You don't say."

"It's a novel actually. Kind of a fantasy thing."

"Fantasy? You mean fiction?" Anne's eyebrows arched above her glasses. "Who needs fiction when you've got science?" she said rhetorically.

"He calls his books 'environmental fiction,'" explained Alice. "He thinks novels are a good way to teach kids about endangered species, you know, like orangutans."

"Well, who knows, he could be right," Anne conceded. "And you've just tagged along for the ride, is that it?"

"It's not as if I had a choice. My parents are divorced and I'm spending this summer with my dad. He thinks traveling to different countries will give me a perspective on the world that I can't get from books."

"Can't argue with that," said Anne. "And you, Shane? What brings you to this part of the world?"

"I'm a foreign exchange student, ma'am," said Shane as he flicked a mosquito off his arm. "And part-time meat wagon for mosquitoes."

Anne smiled. "And you're what, about a junior in high school?"

"Yes, ma'am."

"And you, Alice?"

"I'll be a sophomore in the fall."

"So you're about fourteen?"

"That's right," said Alice.

"And how do you like attending school in Indonesia, Shane?"

"Well ma'am, to tell you the truth, I don't like it all that much."

"Really?" said Anne, surprised that anyone would not enjoy Indonesia. "What don't you like about it?"

"The language barrier knocks me for a loop. All the classes are taught in Indonesian."

"Did you expect them to be taught in English?"

"Well, no, ma'am, of course not. It's just that I don't have a clue about what the teacher is talking about most of the time," said Shane, as he sucked a noodle into his mouth. "I'm really sort of wasting my time here, if you want to know the truth."

"Of course I want to know the truth," said Anne. "I'm a scientist. That's what scientists do."

"What?" said Shane.

"We figure out the truth," said Anne. "Sort out the 'what seems to be' from the 'what is'."

"Oh, right," said Shane.

"You may not have noticed, Shane, but you're in a very interesting part of the world," said Anne. "And Borneo in particular has many truths to reveal. But you have to be open to it. You can't walk around like you've got everything figured out already."

"I know," said Shane. "But the truth is... I'm sort of homesick."

"Many years from now, when you look back on your experiences here, you'll see that it is just a span of time. The important thing to recognize is that you have an opportunity right here and right now. Not many people have the chance to discover and learn about another culture from inside that culture, as you do. You'd be wise to make the most of it."

"I reckon you're right, ma'am, but it's hard for me to concentrate on the good stuff. All I think about is my family and friends back home and how much I miss them. And I wonder how the Giants are doing."

"What I've learned to do, and what's helped me, is to look at my life as if it's a book. Every day I'm on a different page of my life's story. Some pages are interesting and exciting and challenging, and some are just kind of dull, links to the next page. But every day is a new page, and you know what the best thing is?"

"What?" asked Shane and Alice in unison.

"You get to write the book."

"Huh?" said Shane, puckering his lips to suck in a noodle that was slithering from his fork as if it had intentions of its own.

"You're in charge of your own life's story," said Anne. "If you don't like the way it's going, you can change it. Tomorrow you can wake up and say, 'Hey, you know what, I don't like the way things are going, I think I'll start a new chapter.'"

"I have a feeling I started a new chapter today," said Alice.

"I feel like I'm a character in a dang science-fiction book," said Shane. "This has been one of the weirdest days of my life. First I meet Alice here, and that was pretty weird right there. Then all of a sudden I'm a co-conspirator in a plot to free a captive gibbon. Then I get to watch myself do something I just did from, like, outside my body or something. Then I'm carrying on a conversation with an orangutan, and it's, you know, like, okay, and then I find cookies in my backpack that I didn't even put there... what the heck's next, visitors from outer space? Makes me kind of wonder if I should even go to sleep tonight," said Shane.

"Just another beautiful day in paradise, eh?" said Anne.

"Whoa!" said Alice, pushing her stool back from the table so fast it almost tipped over. There, on the floor, crawling as fast as its many hundred magenta legs could carry it, was an invertebrate, a multi-legged creature with a bright red bead-like head and liver-colored body.

"That's a centipede," said Anne. "Give it some room."

"Sucker's as long as a dang hot dog," observed Shane.

"It crawled right over my foot," said Alice, squatting down for a closer look. "Geez, look at the way its legs move, like in little waves or something. It's an optical illusion, almost."

"Yep," said Anne, on her knees next to Alice. "That's definitely a centipede, not a millipede."

"What's the difference?" asked Alice.

"Centipedes have only one pair of legs per body segment, and millipedes have more than one. But the most crucial difference to us is that centipedes are dangerous, and millipedes aren't."

"That's some pretty coordinated coordination," said Shane as he watched the centipede scurry away. Alice and Anne both gave him a what-did-you-say glance.

"Very dangerous," said Iyan. "Not to bite you."

"In the rain forest, creatures that are brightly colored like this guy are often poisonous or dangerous," said Anne. "See how red his head and legs are? That's a warning to other animals to stay away. The red color is also a signal to other animals that he's not very good to eat."

"Maybe I should paint my arms red," said Shane, massaging a mosquito bite.

"How long have you been in Borneo, Ibu Anne?" asked Alice.

"Oh, off and on for the past dozen years," said Anne. "Summers mostly."

"To study orangutans?"

"Yes, that's what I do," said Anne. "I'm very interested in learning how orangutans think. If we can learn how they think—how they process information—we might be able to save them from extinction."

"Extinction?" said Shane. "Aren't these guys pretty far up the food chain for that to happen? I thought only animals like frogs and bugs and little fish no one ever heard of became extinct. You know, critters that don't matter all that much."

"Everything matters, Shane," said Anne. "Even the plants and animals that no one notices play important roles in the earth's ecology and deserve respect and protection. Have you ever heard the term 'background extinction'?"

"Nope," said Shane.

"Background extinction refers to the plants and animals that become extinct naturally," said Anne.

"You mean like the dinosaurs?" asked Alice.

"Right, Alice. No one knows for sure why dinosaurs became extinct, but the research suggests it was from a natural disaster."

"Like an earthquake or a volcano?" said Shane.

"More likely a catastrophic natural disaster, like a meteor crashing into the earth, or an asteroid shower," said Anne.

"Or some kind of gas that poisoned the air," said Shane.

Anne retrieved the notebook from her backpack, tore out a sheet of paper and laid it on the table. She drew two perpendicular lines. "This vertical line represents the number of species that have gone extinct and this horizontal line represents time, going back to the age of dinosaurs at this end and modern day over here at the other end. If we plotted this information, this is how it would look," said Anne, drawing as she spoke. Alice and Shane were surprised when the line Anne drew shot up dramatically as it reached the part of the history timeline that represented the last hundred years.

"Do you see what's happening?" asked Anne.

"Yes, ma'am," said Shane, "and it's scary."

"The number of extinctions has shot way up," said Alice.

"And what do you think the reason for that is?"

"Us," said Shane. "Man. Human beings. That's got to be it."

"You're right, Shane. Man—the earth's most dominant species. In the past few hundred years, since man's tool arsenal has made him more and more efficient in the way he manipulates the earth to suit his own needs, the rate of extinction for the flora and fauna that are in his path of progress has accelerated dramatically."

"Are orangutans really going to become extinct?" asked Alice.

"They're headed in that direction," said Anne gravely. "Unless something happens very soon to reverse the present trend, orangutans could be extinct in the wild in another ten years."

"But how?" asked Alice. "How could that happen?"

"For one thing, there just aren't that many orangutans in the first place. Millions of years ago, orangutans were found all through Asia. Fossilized remains have been found as far north as Vietnam. But over the years, their habitat has decreased and today they are found only on Sumatra and here on Borneo."

"Both of them islands," said Alice.

"Right," said Anne. "At one time, Borneo and Sumatra may have been connected to each other and to the mainland by a land bridge, just as the islands of Java and Bali were once connected. That's one explanation for why we find tigers on both Bali and Java, but don't find them on the island of Lombok, which is only twenty miles away across a channel."

"That's interesting," said Alice thoughtfully. "I wonder why we don't find them on Lombok, too."

"Tigers can swim, but they can't swim very far. They had no way to get to Lombok, that'd be my guess," said Anne.

"Are the orangutans on Sumatra the same as the orangutans on Borneo?" asked Shane.

"They're a related subspecies, yes, but with some slight variations. Sumatra males don't tend to have prominent cheek pads, but the Borneo orangutans do. And Borneo orangutans tend to be more of a dark, chocolate color. Orangutans in Sumatra are more copper-colored."

"When we were following Nik today, I noticed he was kind of purple, sort of an eggplant color," said Shane.

"Nik's from the northeast," said Anne. "They're a little darker up there. The other reason Nik looks a little purple is that in the rain forest, the leaves reflect green light, but absorb red light before it reaches the understory. Not much of it reaches the forest floor. Orangutans don't have that bright, red-orange cast unless they're sitting in a pool of sunlight."

"What are human beings doing that is causing the orangutans to go extinct?" asked Alice.

"Well, the answer to that question is very complicated, but the short answer is deforestation, loss of habitat," said Anne. "They're cutting down the lowland forest, which is prime orangutan habitat. The orangutans have nowhere to live."

"But when my dad and I flew over Borneo, I looked out the window and saw nothing but trees, trees and more trees," said Alice. "And a whole bunch of brown rivers."

"It's true that there still is some intact primary forest in Borneo. But if you had looked carefully at the trees as the plane descended, you'd have seen that many of them were planted in rows."

"Orchards?" said Alice.

"Plantations. Oil palm, rubber trees, bananas, rice paddies," said Anne. "More and more all the time. Did you notice any patches of cleared land?"

"Yes, I did," said Alice. "Patches of bare red and yellow dirt."

"Clear cutting is supposed to be against the law in Borneo," said Anne. "The problem wouldn't be so bad if the forests were logged responsibly so that when they were finished there would still be enough intact forest remaining to support the plants and animals that live here."

"It's hard to imagine that there are all these problems going on in a place like Borneo. I mean, this is the remotest place I've ever seen," said Shane.

"Borneo may seem remote to you, Shane," said Anne, "but it's really not. Indonesia is made up of 17,000 islands, and in terms of population, it is the fourth largest country in the world. And that's a pretty high population density."

"Wow, fourth," said Alice. "I didn't know that."

"I did," said Shane. "I had to bone up on Indonesia before I came here. Only China, India and the United States have more people than Indonesia."

"Borneo and Sumatra are the third and fourth largest islands in the world, but compared with North America or the African continent, they're pretty small places. In most places in Indonesia, there are a lot of people trying to live on very little land," said Anne. "In Borneo, the land is so nutrient poor that it can't support large populations of human beings. That's why this island is not as populated as some of the others, such as Java and Bali, for example."

"I see what you mean about this being a complicated problem," said Shane.

"The problem," said Anne, "is that there are too many people and they are having way too many babies. When I arrived this year I read in the *Jakarta Post* that 450 Indonesian children die every day from malnutrition. Think about that for a minute."

Alice did the math in her head and said, "That's like over 160,000 children dying a year. Can that be right?"

"Can you imagine those kinds of numbers anywhere in North America?" said Anne.

"People would freak," said Alice. "No one would stand for it."

"You'd think that with so many children dying, people would wise up and stop having so many babies," said Shane.

"You'd think so," said Anne, shaking her head, "but they keep on popping them out like there's no tomorrow. The children who survive have to live somewhere and eat something. So more and more land is cleared for human use, for houses, farms, cities, roads, office buildings. And of course when all these children grow up they'll need jobs, a lot of jobs, and that means more factories, more mines, more timber cutting—more consumption of natural resources."

"And less forest for orangutans," said Alice.

"Cutting down the forests is a big problem in the U.S., too," said Shane.

"Up where I used to live in Humboldt County, there was this woman named Julia Butterfly Hill who lived in a giant redwood tree for like two years," said Alice. "She figured as long as she was living in Luna, they couldn't cut it down."

"Luna?" said Shane.

"That's what she called her redwood tree."

"She named a tree?" said Shane.

"Well, you know, they do things like that in Humboldt County," said Alice.

"So what happened?" said Shane.

"The lumber company that owned the land agreed not to cut down Luna, and to leave a buffer zone of trees around Luna," said Alice.

"Brave young woman, I think I'd like her—and I like that she gave the redwood tree a name," said Anne, smiling as she imagined a young woman living high in a tree, arboreal, like an orangutan. "It's impossible to overstate what a huge problem forest mismanagement is in Borneo. Loss of habitat is the number-one problem as far as the orangutan population is concerned."

"What's the solution?" said Shane.

"Can't the government just put a stop to it?" said Alice.

"They could," said Anne, "but they don't. Politicians don't think about preserving the forests or the animals. They are not farsighted enough to realize the consequences of their policies. It's all a matter of money to politicians."

"What do you mean?" asked Shane.

"Well, let's say there's a foreign businessman who needs wood, a lot of wood. And let's say he has a friend in the government who knows a high-ranking official in the Indonesian Ministry of Forestry. He might say, 'Listen, my good friend, if you let my company come in and log your rain forest, I'll see that you and your family are rewarded handsomely.'"

"Can they do that?" asked Alice.

"The Indonesian people are told this is a great deal for them because they'll have jobs felling trees for forty dollars a month, or working in the lumber mill that the foreign investor has so generously built." Anne sighed deeply, as she was prone to do whenever she talked about how the orangutans were losing their habitat. "Few people in the government really care enough to try to put a halt to the destruction, but the multinational corporations who come in and cut down the forests, they're the real culprits."

"How many orangutans do you reckon are left, you know, in the wild?" asked Shane.

"No one really knows for sure," said Anne. "Many different researchers collect data, set up transects, count nests, count orangutans, estimate the reproductive rate and weigh that against the survival rate, and come up with some kind of educated guess."

"So what's the best guess?" said Alice.

"About 15,000 on both Borneo and Sumatra, maybe substantially less after the fires of the past couple of years get factored into the equation."

Shane shrugged. "Is that a lot? Or a little?"

"Think of it this way," said Anne. "If you put one wild orangutan on every one of Indonesia's 17,000 islands, you'd probably run out of orangutans before you ran out of islands. That's how few are left in the wild."

"That's scary," said Alice.

"Here's another way to look at it," said Shane. "Remember a couple of summers ago when Mark McGwire broke the home run record?"

"I remember that," said Alice.

"There were 60,000 people in the stadium that night. If every one of those 15,000 orangutans left in the wild had attended that game, I don't think they would have even filled the cheap seats."

"Excellent analogy," said Anne. "It helps to put these numbers into a perspective that has meaning to people."

Alice stifled a yawn and said, "I sure am sleepy all of a sudden."

"Well," said Anne, "it is dark. All the orangutans have long since bedded down for the night, and it's about time for us to do the same. You each have your own room. Alice, you can sleep in the room next to the kitchen, and Shane, you can have the one Julia Roberts slept in when she was here for a visit."

"Julia Roberts?" said Shane. "For real?"

"Of course for real. Don't you watch TV?" Anne said as Shane ran down the hall to inspect his room, which now had celebrity status.

"Hey," yelled Shane when he reached the room. "There's four bunks in here, which one did she sleep in?"

"Shane!" Alice whispered hoarsely. "Can't you just talk in a normal voice? Please?"

"Got to yell to be heard over all these bugs," said Shane.

"You're just like Bento," said Anne. "Hormonally challenged."

"Bento?" said Alice. "Who's Bento?"

"He's one of the subadult orangutans I have been observing. I'd like to be at Bento's nest when he wakes up in the morning, otherwise I'll never find him. If you like, you two can come with me."

"That'd be cool," said Shane.

"I'd like to see what a scientist does out in the forest," said Alice.

"Well, I'm afraid you'll find it's not all that exciting, but you're welcome to tag along if you like. I'll wake you at five," said Anne.

"Five?" said Shane. "But it'll still be dark."

"As I said, you've got to recognize opportunities when they present themselves, even in the dark. Goodnight."

"Good night, Anne," said Alice. "And thanks for a good page."

"And for the mosquito netting," said Shane.

The Follow

It was still pitch-black when Alice opened her sleep-filled eyes. She could barely distinguish the milky haze of the mosquito netting that hung protectively over her bed. Her first sleepy thought was that there was a ghost in the room. She had no idea what time it was, but then she had no idea what time she had retired the night before, either. The silver hands of her watch still pointed straight up. This whole concept of life without time, or of time standing still, or stretching, or whatever trick it was playing on her, was beginning to appeal to her. As faint gray light seeped into the room and more details emerged from its dark corners, she thought of her father, and worried that he would be frantic when he returned and found her gone. Why hadn't she thought to leave him a note? Surely he would have returned to the guesthouse by now. Or would he have? Did the veil of suspended time hanging over her adventure with Shane extend to her father as well? Was he seeing her and talking with her, even though she was here, not there? Or was she there, and it was really here where she was not? Was all this a dream? It seemed so real—Shane, Nik, Yayat, Siti and that pesky hornbill, Sarijan. And Anne, she was real. She wasn't a dream, was she?

A faint scratching at the wooden windowsill drew Alice from her dreamy reverie. There, standing upright and cloaked in the faint light of a new day, was one of the oddest-looking creatures she had ever seen. The animal was no bigger than a Beanie Baby, and was covered with fine, pale gray-brown fur. Its hairless tail, about as long as its body was tall, was as thin as the cord that connected the mouse to Alice's computer back home. At the tip of the tail was a tuft of coarse hair that made it seem as if the diminutive creature was dragging around a paintbrush. The pads on the bony fingers of its dainty hands were round, and seemed too big for the fingers. If this creature's hands were as big as Alice's, it would look as if it had tennis balls impaled on it finger tips. Opposite the pad of what would have to be called its index finger was an opposable thumb, and this, Alice knew, meant that the animal was a primate. Like each of its fingers, its thumb had a nail. But on the second and third toes of its feet there were claws instead of nails. Alice had seen animals with nails, like orangutans, gibbons and chimpanzees; and animals with claws, like coyotes and wolves and her beloved Scottish terrier, Kirby; but here on her windowsill was an animal that, unless her eyes deceived her, had both. Its head was the size of a cue ball, but shaped more like a chicken egg. The little creature's ears were pointed like a squirrel's, but inside them, the skin was ribbed, as if they had evolved to extract every wave of sound from the animal's surroundings. Two nostrils flared on either side of its narrow nose and its mouth was set in a serene, Buddha-like smile. But its most distinguishing characteristic by far was the pair of dime-size, bright yellow eyes that dominated its face. What kind of evolutionary time warp did you get caught in? wondered Alice, just as a knock came at the door.

"Alice, Shane, time to hit the trail. Ten minutes," called Anne. Alice could hear her go back down the wooden walkway outside the room.

"I'm up," said Alice, turning toward the door. When she turned back, the little animal had vanished. She hurried to her window and caught a glimpse of the little creature leaping from branch to branch. Then it was gone, swallowed by the darkness of the pre-dawn forest.

Alice lay back in bed, closed her eyes a moment, and listened to the morning sounds of the rain forest. Not far from camp, a gibbon greeted the day. Its high-pitched, bubbling melody drifted up through the canopy and floated over the tops of the trees. From farther away, a reply floated back on the morning mist. Alice wondered how she would ever describe this song of the gibbons to her friends back at school. It would be as hopeless as trying to explain what rock music sounded like to someone whose only musical reference was Beethoven. She guessed she would say it was like air bubbles rising through water, and in each bubble was trapped a single note that was released when the bubble burst upon the surface. Or maybe it wasn't exactly like that. It was, she decided on further consideration, an indescribable sound, one that had no comparison in her range of experiences and one that her friends would be hard-pressed to imagine. But the song of the Indian cuckoo that had also chimed in was easy to describe: four identical mid-octave notes played on a woodwind instrument, simple, elegant, clear and beautiful. A song any child could play without a lesson.

"C'mon, Alice," called Shane, "Anne's waiting."

A hundred yards from camp, a ten-yard swath of silt-choked yellow water flowed lazily through the forest. A thick steel cable was suspended over the nameless river and anchored on the far side in a hole someone had chiseled through the foot-thick, fin-like buttress of a giant dipterocarp. The other end of the cable was wrapped around a tree trunk on the side of the river where Alice, Shane and Anne now stood. Suspended from the cable was a two-seat gondola made of angle iron and sheet metal. The gondola had at one time been painted a bright yellow, but most of the paint had worn off, exposing the raw metal which was now rusting. Ropes tied to corners of the gondola led to pulleys on the riverbank, so that the gondola passengers could pull on one rope to get across the river and on the other to return.

On the far side of the river, a large male orangutan squatted on his haunches, waiting patiently for Anne and her entourage to cross. Bento was a dusty eggplant-colored male with the swollen suggestion of cheekpads emerging from either side of his broad, flat face. Above Bento a scrawny juvenile orangutan clutched a slender ulin trunk like a treed raccoon.

"Bento's up early this morning," said Anne. "And there is Gomez up there above him. He's one of our new releases."

"How old is Bento?" asked Shane, suspecting he was about his own age.

"No way of knowing for sure, but he's probably ten or eleven," said Anne. "A subadult."

"How about the little guy?" said Alice.

"Gomez is a juvenile, probably four or five."

"Scrawny little dude," said Shane.

"He's having a tough time of it," said Anne, looking at Gomez through her binoculars. "He hangs around the camp hoping for handouts. Last week he stole a package of noodles and ran into the forest to eat them, but a wild boar came charging out of the bush and stole them from him."

"Dang!" said Shane. "A wild boar?"

"Gomez was so angry he ran up a tree and shook the branches for fifteen minutes." Anne handed the binoculars to Alice. "See how thin he is, and how dull his hair is compared with Bento's?"

"Yes," said Alice, bringing Gomez into focus. She passed the binos to Shane so he could look, too.

"Looks like he just got out of prison," said Shane.

"You could say that," said Anne. "Come on, let's cross."

Bento wandered a few paces up the trail, then waited for Anne and the children. Watching Bento migrate toward the forest made Gomez feel safer. Hooking his thin fingers around the ulin trunk, which was about the diameter of a tuna can, he placed one foot below the other and made his way down. When he reached the forest floor he climbed into the cable car and sat there as if expecting it to move. Shane isolated Gomez in his camera's viewfinder and when Gomez scowled, he pressed the shutter button.

"Got it!" said the young photographer.

When he realized the cable car wasn't going to move on its own, Gomez climbed out and swung hand over hand along the suspension cable toward the opposite river bank. Halfway across, he stopped and hung suspended by his feet and hands. His protruding potbelly made Alice think of a bag of clothespins hanging on the line.

"Got that one, too!" said Shane. "This is really cool!"

"When an orangutan swings hand over hand like that it's called brachiating," said Anne, "though they don't do it all that much in the forest."

"Why not?" asked Alice.

"They're too heavy, especially the males," said Anne. "Vegetation that is not busy growing is busy decaying, and sometimes it's hard to tell the difference. Most orangutans have been unpleasantly surprised when a limb they think will hold them breaks."

When Gomez reached the other side of the river, he sprinted up another tree and as the tree started to bend under his weight, he began to rock back and forth. He pressed his thin lips together and made an uncomplimentary raspberry sound that seemed directed at Shane and his camera.

Both Shane and Alice laughed at the noise and Shane said, "What's that all about?"

"Could be a reaction to you," said Anne. "He's never seen you before."

"People usually don't have that kind of reaction to me until they know me better," said Shane.

"Or, it could be that he's just glad to get away from Bento."

"He's afraid of Bento?" asked Alice.

"Intimidated is more like it," said Anne. "I was hoping Gomez and Bento would become friends and pal around together. Bento could teach Gomez how to find food in the forest. But it doesn't look like that's going to happen any time soon. Bento's King of the Forest, and all the other orangutans know it. You don't see Nik hanging around today, do you? He's probably hiding out someplace."

"Interesting," said Alice, watching Gomez hanging from a liana by one long arm, "this orangutan society."

"Yes," said Anne, "they're a fascinating bunch. And the more I learn about them the more fascinating they become."

Once across the river, Alice and Shane followed Anne, who in turn followed Bento, giving the orangutan plenty of room in front of her. In the lead, Bento followed nothing more than his whim. With no one to meet and no appointments to keep, he established a leisurely pace as he crabbed up the steep path.

"I call this Granny Hiking," said Anne. "Just a morning stroll through the woods."

"Just as well," said Shane, mopping his brow with his bandanna. "I'm already sweating buckets."

"It gets easier, Shane," said Anne, whose thick khaki shirt was soaked through with perspiration. "Once we reach the ridge the trail flattens out a bit."

Bento plucked a rattan shoot, then moseyed along the trail as if he hadn't a care in the world. When he reached the ridge he paused at the base of a kledang

Here's Gomez, trying to hitch a ride across the river in the cable car. S.B.

tree. A wrinkle crossed his brow as he pondered his next move for a moment. Then he began to climb. Twenty feet above the forest floor, Bento squatted on a limb whose ability to support his weight seemed questionable. But once situated and confident in the selection of his lofty perch, he stripped a bacon-size piece of bark from the underside of the very limb that supported him and drew it through his clenched teeth to extract the juices.

"He's eating bark," said Alice, looking at Bento through Anne's binoculars.

"He's after the nutrients in the cambium layer just below the outer bark," said Anne. "He's likes the sap, too—it's good stuff, loaded with nutrients."

When a piece of half-chewed bark floated to the forest floor, Shane picked it up. "Looks pretty, you know, woody," he said, peeling a strip with his teeth and chewing it.

"Fibrous," said Anne.

"How's it taste?" asked Alice.

"You know when you're eating an ice cream bar and you get down to the stick?" said Shane. "It tastes like the stick."

"Shane, you might not want to stand right under Bento like that," Anne

Here's Gomez again, doing his best imitation of a clothespin bag. S.B.

warned. "He had terrible diarrhea yesterday."

"Whoa," said Shane, backing off a few paces, "thanks for the warning. I know what that's like. I had the runs for two weeks straight when I first got here."

"Sometimes it takes our digestive tracts that long to acclimate to a new diet," said Anne. "But in Bento's case, I suspect it was all the figs he ate yesterday."

Suddenly there was a loud snap followed by a thud, a grunt and the sound of Bento's body rolling like a runaway truck tire down through the tangle of vines and ferns into the gully. Anne peered down the ravine to see if Bento was all right. Bento looked up at her with his intelligent brown eyes, somewhat surprised but mostly embarrassed that he, the undisputed King of the Forest, had been caught in such a position.

"Bento isn't aware of his own weight," said Anne. "A lot of the rehabilitated orangutans aren't."

"You mean they can't judge whether a branch is going to be strong enough to hold them?" asked Alice.

"For a lot of them, the last time they were in the forest was when they were babies and could climb just about anything without fear," said Anne. "But then

Bento, the undisputed King of the Forest and all-around cool dude. S.B.

they were poached, and who knows what happened to them after that. Eventually the fortunate ones end up at the rehab center and spend a few years learning the survival skills they would have learned from their mothers, though I can't say that a weight-awareness program is high on the agenda. When they are released in the forest, in their minds they're still infants, and they climb the first tree they see, just as they remember doing when they were young. They don't take into account that they now weigh eighty or ninety pounds and the little saplings they climbed as babies can no longer support their weight."

"That's got to be quite an adjustment," said Alice.

"A couple of the rehabs have actually fallen out of trees and broken their arms," said Anne. "Fortunately they were under observation at the time and the technicians were able to get them back to the clinic and have their broken bones set."

"But what if no one had found them?" asked Shane.

"They could have died from their injuries, or their bones might not have mended properly and they could have ended up crippled, which would prevent them from foraging or successfully competing for food with other orangutans."

Bento stood and brushed the dried leaves from his hairy arms, then rambled down the slope, away from the predictable ridge trail. Each step Bento took led the team of followers deeper into a world of shadows upon shadows, a mosaic of depths and false depths where each foot needed to be planted carefully before the next step was taken. The forest floor was a sea of light-seeking foliage with pointed leaves, and hidden beneath that were twine-like shoots that twisted this way and that, their pale trails a history of the sun's path.

With her attention focused on Bento and not on her next step, Alice tripped on one of the hidden vines and was thrown to the ground.

Shane rushed to her side. "You okay?"

"Yeah," said Alice, brushing herself off.

"Man, this is like trying to wade through a field of shoelaces," said Shane, pulling back a fern to let Alice pass.

When they caught up to Bento he was squatting next to a rattan plant, chewing its flavorful stalks contentedly. Anne, Alice and Shane took the opportunity to rest against a sturdy dipterocarp buttress and enjoy the peaceful serenity of the forest. Then, from off in the distance, came a sound unlike any they'd heard that day.

"What the heck is that?" said Shane. "Sounds like someone's roaring through the woods on a dirt bike."

"That's not a dirt bike, Shane," said Alice. "Don't you recognize that sound? It's hornbills. Don't you remember Sarijan?"

"Sounds like something's disturbed them," said Anne. "Maybe a predator."

"A predator?" said Shane. "Like what?"

"A clouded leopard, maybe, or a civet cat, though they generally hunt at night."

"I'd sure hate to be living next door to them and have to listen to that racket all the time," said Shane. "I'd never get any sleep."

"When you sit quietly in the rain forest like this," said Alice, "it kind of reminds you of the city. I mean all the chirps and trills that the birds and insects make. It's like the whole forest is a motor."

"It is like a motor, Alice. And wouldn't it be tragic if one day the motor stopped running?" said Anne wistfully.

When Bento finished his rattan snack, he dropped the chewed stalks and

Bento dropped this piece of bark for me to try. It wasn't that bad. S.B.

made his way to a slow-moving creek at the bottom of the ravine. Using his arms for support, he lowered his body to the water as if about to do a pushup. Then he lowered his head to the water, extended his rubbery lips and drank deeply. When his thirst was quenched, he splashed through the shallow water and up the opposite bank.

"Looks like it's uphill for a while," said Anne, setting off in pursuit with Alice and Shane in tow. A few minutes later Bento discovered a fallen log on the forest floor, five feet in diameter and fifty feet long. The giant tree had fallen decades ago and was slowly returning to the earth in a timeless ballet of decay.

Bento spied a pool of sunlight near the center of the log and stretched out on the soft bark for an after-lunch nap.

"Might as well get comfy," said Anne. "We may be here for a while."

Anne, Alice and Shane staked out perches of their own and sat down.

"So this is what following an orangutan is all about," said Alice.

"A lot of ups and downs and a lot of sitting around," said Shane, mopping the sweat from his brow with his shirt sleeves.

"It's definitely not for everyone," said Anne, as she pulled a small notebook

Here are some rattan stalks that Bento left behind. S.B.

from her fanny pack and scribbled a few notes. "A lot of time they'll just sit in a tree for hours and eat fruit. Sometimes they'll do something interesting, display some sort of behavior I've never seen before, and that's what makes all the waiting worthwhile for me."

Twenty minutes later, Bento awoke from his nap. Still groggy with sleep, he yawned, stretched his long arms, and then suddenly rolled off the log and onto the forest floor with a leaf-rustling thud, his second clumsy mishap of the day. He stood up slowly and shook his head, then bolted suddenly up the hill like a rock star trying to elude adoring fans. When he spotted a ten-foot-tall bandang tree, a forest palm standing alone among the taller trees like a misplaced Roman column, he stopped in his tracks. The bandang tree, Anne told Alice and Shane, was one of the orangutan's favorite foods, and one of the most difficult to get access to. At the top of the trunk, protected by an array of spiny fronds, was the umbut, the succulent heart of the bandang.

"Let's wait here and watch," said Anne. "I want to see how Bento will solve this problem."

Bento looked to where he wanted to be, which was atop the bandang, and

After lunch, there's nothing like a siesta. S.B.

surveyed the nearby trees. He selected a thin dipterocarp a few yards away and began to climb. When the tree started to bend under his weight, he rocked back and forth, building momentum. When the arc of the tree carried him over the top of the palm, he released his grip, dropping like a pole-vaulter. He stood triumphantly at the top of the bandang like a real life Mighty Joe Young, having completely avoided the sharp fronds that were the bandang's defense against predators like him. He began to divide the shoots at the top of the palm into small subsections and pull them out one at a time. When the shoots broke off too short, Bento stood up and scratched his skull thoughtfully while he considered a solution to this new problem. He solved it by folding over the tips of the subsections to make them stronger. Now when he pulled, the juicy tips came out intact. He settled in to enjoy the delicious, succulent heart of the bandang palm.

"That was amazing," said Alice, "the way he figured out how to do that."

"Yes," agreed Anne, "that was a sign of orangutan intelligence."

"Did that pole-vaulting stuff count as using tools?"

"It comes very close."

"That guy's a geometry whiz," agreed Shane. "And a great athlete."

"Okay," whispered Anne. "Let's head back to camp. He'll be eating for ten minutes or so, and we need to get a head start on him in case he decides to follow us."

"That'd be a switch," said Shane.

"It is one thing to follow an orangutan, especially one as big and powerful as Bento, but quite another to be followed."

"Why?" asked Alice. "Is he dangerous?"

"He's unpredictable, and that makes him dangerous. He's an adolescent and he's strong. With orangutans, especially the large adolescent males, you always want to be the follower, not the followee."

CHAPTER 11

Uce's Gift

After the morning's follow and observation of Bento, the three Homo sapiens returned to camp for lunch and to discuss what direction their adventure would now take. Alice and Shane had yet to meet the Old Man of the Forest, but they had neither seen nor heard from their escort Nik since he left them in Anne's care the previous evening. But they were having such a good time with Anne, tramping through the forest and learning about orangutans, that perhaps their introduction to the Old Man could wait another day.

While they were off in the forest, the picnic table where they dined the night before had been transformed into Iyan's field office. They found him transferring data from his field notebook to a laptop computer. Here in this remote camp, miles from electricity feeds, the laptop received power from a generator whose muffled hum could be heard sputtering from a shed nestled into a thicket behind the camp. Iyan had classified more than thirty individual trees that grew in this particular part of the forest. The common bond of Iyan's trees, the one aspect that linked them, was that each provided nourishment for the orangutans. Alice and Shane peeked over Iyan's shoulder at his list. Each tree was referenced by family, genus, and species, and by its vernacular, or common, name. Iyan had

When I saw this leaf upon a leaf upon a leaf, it kind of said "biodiversity." S.B.

also created a column for remarks. At a glance it was easy to see that the bandang tree, whose tasty heart Bento lusted after at brunch, was a member of the palm family. Its genus was Borassodendron; its species, borneensis. Under the remark column, Iyan noted that orangutans ate not only its fruit, but the heart of the palm, the umbut, as well.

"Cempedak," said Shane, reading over Iyan's shoulder. "I kind of like the sound of that one. Looks like the orangutans put it to good use—they eat, what, the bark, sap, cambium and fruit, and the young leaves. Seems like they eat just about everything but the roots."

"Does anyone know how many species of trees there are on Borneo?" Alice wondered.

"No one knows the exact number, but thousands, it's safe to say, Miss Alice," said Iyan, whose command of English, though not completely fluent, was far superior to Alice's knowledge of Indonesian. "Borneo is rich in biodiversity," Iyan continued. "Scientists discover new species of plants and animals all the time."

"You know something," said Alice, "I've been noticing how many Indonesians speak a little English, but hardly any Americans speak Indonesian."

"Same thing with Mexicans," said Shane. "A lot of them speak English, but not that many gringos speak Spanish."

"I guess people learn what they have to in order to survive," said Alice. "That says something about Americans, doesn't it? But I'm not sure what."

"I guess it says that Americans don't have to speak other languages to get along, so they don't bother to learn them. We just expect people to speak English if they want to talk to us," said Shane.

"How arrogant," said Alice. "Iyan, have you ever discovered a new plant?"

Iyan laughed. "Oh, not me, Miss Alice. I am just learning about all the plants that grow in the forest. One day I hope to be a botanist, or a conservation biologist, or a primate psychologist like Ibu Anne, and help the people of Indonesia understand how important forests are to our country." said Iyan. Then he added, "And to our well-being."

"You flatter me, Iyan," said Anne. She looked at Alice and Shane and said, "Iyan already knows more about Borneo plant life than do most people who have been studying botany on this island for years. I look at Iyan and see how comfortable he is in the forest and how quickly he learns the relationships between the plants and animals, and I think it's going to be Iyan's destiny to help change the world with his knowledge of the ecosystem."

"Maybe so, Ibu Anne," said Iyan, closing down his laptop, "with your help."

"One of the most extraordinary characteristics of a tropical rain forest is its biodiversity," said Anne, shifting the focus of the conversation away from her. "When the forest is razed, and, say, a palm oil or rubber tree plantation is planted in its place, that diversity, that variety of native plant and animal life, is lost forever, and with it, its secrets. Perhaps growing from a decaying deadfall near an unnamed stream in the mountainous heart of Borneo is an undiscovered fungus that holds the key to the cure of many diseases. Or maybe we'll learn that combining a fungus from Borneo with the skin of a frog found only at the Amazon headwaters in Ecuador will result in a cure for cancer, or Alzheimer's, or the HIV virus and AIDS. Who knows what's still there to be discovered on the inner frontiers of this planet? And who among us is smart or farsighted enough to calculate the value of what we do not yet know? Not the lumber com-

Uce, the proud new mother. S.B.

panies or the plantation owners, that's for sure." Anne pulled a stray wisp of wiry red hair from the corner of her mouth and sighed. "But at the rate the earth's forests are being destroyed, we may never know whether a particular lichen in Bolivia, or the nectar of some rare orchid in Peru, or the cambium layer of that bark we saw Bento chewing on today, hold medicinal secrets or not."

Just then a small female orangutan with long, glowing orange hair and a tiny infant clinging to her body appeared at the edge of the clearing that defined the camp. "Ibu Anne, look!" said Iyan. "It is Uce!"

"My God, it is Uce... and look who she's got with her!" said Anne. "A baby!"

Anne rummaged through her backpack for her camera and, with Iyan at her side, cautiously approached the shy new mother. Sensing the significance of the occasion, Shane and Alice hung back a few paces and looked at each other, silently acknowledging their good fortune.

"Alice, Shane, what we have here before us is truly a triumph of nature over man," said Anne, her voice breaking with emotion. "Uce was the orangutan responsible for starting the rehabilitation center. Ten years ago, a man named Willie was offered her in a marketplace in Balikpapan. She was an infant, and in terrible shape, dehydrated, malnourished, in shock and a day or two away from death. Willie brought her home and his children helped nurse her back to health." Soon after that, Anne went on, Willie was offered a second orphan, then a third. He soon figured out that the infant orangutans available on the streets of Balikpapan were indicators of a much larger problem: the black-market pet trade. The baby orangutans rescued by Willie and cared for by his family soon captivated the hearts of the students at his children's school, the international school in Balikpapan. Caring for baby orangutans became their focus, too. "Then, once the students got their parents involved," Anne said, "the orangutan project gained momentum and just took off. And that's how the orangutan rehabilitation center got its start."

"Wow," said Alice, impressed. "You mean kids started it?"

"That's right, kids," said Anne, unable to take her eyes from Uce, who apparently had the same reaction to Anne. "Look how healthy she looks—her hair is so thick and shiny. But what is extraordinary is that Uce hasn't been seen in several years and here she is with a baby—and after all she's been through."

"I wonder who the father is?" said Iyan.

"Could be Charlie, I suppose," said Anne.

"Panjul, perhaps," said Iyan.

"What this birth indicates," said Anne, "is that Uce is succeeding in her new life."

"She's dating," said Shane. "That's for sure."

"We already know that rehabbed orangutans can survive on their own, but this is the first baby born in this forest. Uce has shown us that rehabbed orangutans can reproduce as well." Anne turned to look at Alice and Shane. "You have no idea what a momentous event this birth is."

"I think I'm getting an idea," whispered Alice.

"This is better than, than…" said Shane pulling his camera from his backpack. "Dang! I can't think of anything better than this."

Uce broke a leaf off a nearby palm and offered it to Anne. Anne brushed a tear from her eye as she accepted Uce's gift. "Nine years ago," said Anne, "after Willie rescued Uce and brought her back to the forest, he gave her a palm leaf, a leaf from the very same species of palm," said Anne, softly fingering the edge of the leaf. "She remembers."

"How old are orangutans before they start having babies?" asked Alice, watching the infant as it suckled Uce's breast.

"Oh, they're kind of like teenagers," said Anne. "They start experimenting with sex early on, when they're four or five. But it's more play than anything serious. Playing is one way orangutans learn about their world. But to answer your question, females don't become sexually mature, that is to say, able to reproduce, until they are in their mid-teens."

"I read somewhere that an orangutan in a zoo gave birth when she was only seven," said Alice.

"That may very well be true," said Anne. "In zoos, females have been known to deliver offspring at seven or eight. But keep in mind, a zoo is an artificial environment that bears little resemblance to an orangutan's natural habitat. In zoos, the maturing process is accelerated. The behavior of captive orangutans is quite different from the behavior of their wild kin."

"What about the males," asked Shane. "How old are they before they, you know, get interested?"

"Males don't reach sexual maturity until they are about twenty or so. Some subadult males, like our friends Bento and Nik, do copulate with females and there is genetic evidence that subadults actually have produced offspring. Sometimes subadults copulate with females whether the females want to or not."

"You mean they *rape* them?" asked Alice, a dark furrow of doubt etched in her forehead.

"Humans aren't the only species that rape," said Anne. "In fact, orangutans are quite well known for their sexual aggression."

"Whoa," said Alice. "That's kind of shocking. I thought animals were kinder to each other than humans are to one another."

"Yes, it is shocking when you look at rape through the eyes of a human being," said Anne. "But with the great apes, it may actually serve a purpose."

"Like what?" asked Alice.

"Like getting as many females pregnant as possible," said Anne. "Maybe they have a sense that they are losing the battle for survival, who knows? Of course, another reason is intimidation."

"Intimidation?" said Alice.

"Well, if a female can be intimidated into not resisting a male's sexual advances while she and he are young, maybe she won't resist later on."

"Geez," said Alice.

"So, how long do these guys live, anyway?" asked Shane.

"We are still collecting data on the longevity of orangutans. Scientists have only been studying them seriously since the early 1970s, and at that time thirty or thirty-five years was our best guess," said Anne. "But some of the orangutans that were mature when we first started studying them are still going strong."

"You mean they're over forty now?" said Shane.

"Yes, some of them are. We've had to revise our longevity hypothesis upward. We now think orangutans might live fifty or sixty years, maybe longer. That's getting right up there with how long humans live, at least in some Third World nations, like Indonesia."

"Yeah," said Alice. "The bellhop at one of the hotels we stayed in asked my dad how old he was and when my dad said he was fifty-four, the bellhop said that was how old his father was when he died."

"Serious bummer," said Shane.

"But, Anne, if females don't start having babies until they are fifteen, how many do they have during their lifetime?" asked Alice.

"The answer to that question, Alice, speaks volumes about the reason orangutans are threatened with extinction," said Anne. "The reproductive cycle of orangutans is very slow. The number of babies orangutans have varies from individual to individual, but generally speaking, a female will produce only three or four offspring during her lifetime."

"Dang," said Shane. "They're not exactly rabbits, are they?"

"Not exactly like rabbits, or mice, or bats or civets or any other animal with a high rate of reproduction," said Anne. "You see, an orangutan stays with its mother for eight to ten years. During that time the young orangutan learns how to survive in the forest, which, believe me, is no easy trick. The youngsters learn how to get at favorite foods such as the bandang, as we watched Bento do this morning, or the even more difficult nibung. Their mothers show them where to find termites, and show them the right kinds of bark to eat. Orangutans are very creative, but they don't do a lot of experimenting on their own, at least not when it comes to food. They depend mostly on their mothers to teach them, but they learn from other orangutans, too."

"Just as kids learn from each other?" said Alice.

"Yes, orangutans swap information just as kids do, and they tend to develop specialized talents."

"What do you mean, 'specialized talents'?" asked Shane.

"Well, one orangutan might be very good at opening termite nests. Another's specialty might be getting honey out of a hive. Maybe he's discovered a special technique, maybe a way to use sticks to get at the honey that's way down in the hive. The other orangutans see him doing this and a light comes on in their minds and then they give it a try, and in that way the information is passed along from orangutan to orangutan. So, helping the orangutans make friends with each other while they are in rehab is one way we can help ensure their survival on their own in the forest. It is important that orangutans become resources to each other." Anne pushed her glasses, which had begun to slip, back onto the bridge of her nose. "Teaching the orphans survival skills they would have learned—should have learned—from their mothers is the greatest challenge we face in the rehabilitation process."

"It's like someone needs to adopt them and be their mother," said Alice.

"That's right, Alice, but if we expect orphaned orangutans to survive in the forest, we must find new and better methods to teach them the skills they would have learned from their mothers."

"I guess so," said Alice, "But how do you do that?"

Anne sighed and said, "It's very, very difficult. The way things are now, the orphans come into the rehab center and, if they pass quarantine, they are placed in socialization cages with a lot of other orphans. There, we hope, some lifelong friendships will be born. The orangutans get fed some natural foods, like leaves and bark, but those foods are very hard to come by. I mean, it's not as if you can go to the market and buy a truckload of ulin leaves or wild figs. We're working on ways to obtain more wild fruits to feed the orangutans. Right now, unfortunately, the bulk of their diet consists of food that is convenient and available to us, but is not available in the forest."

"Like what?" asked Shane.

"Milk, rice, bananas, papaya, mangos—all of which you'd find in a market or in a farmer's garden, but not in the forest."

"So how do you get them to recognize the kind of foods they would find in the forest?" asked Alice.

"Therein lies one big problem," said Anne, holding an index finger in the still air. "That's why, since we've discovered how hard it is for orangutans to learn about forest foods, we've added a new link to our rehabilitation program."

"What new link?" asked Alice.

"A Halfway House."

"A Halfway House?" said Shane. "Like where people go to live when they get out of prison?"

"Same principle," said Anne, "but more of a Halfway Forest, really. The way things are now, the orangutans spend three or four years in rehab and then they're released, sometimes in great numbers, into the forest."

"Then what happens to them?" said Alice.

Anne shrugged. "Some of them, like Bento and Gomez and a handful of the others, hang around the release sites because they know that if things get tough, they'll get handouts."

"Does that count as a survival skill?" asked Shane rhetorically.

"But Bento knows how to find food," said Alice. "We watched him."

"Right, but he's the exception, not the rule," said Anne. "It's the others, the ones that aren't hanging around, that I'm concerned about."

"So, what do you think happens to them?" said Shane. "They don't just disappear, do they?"

"Nobody knows for sure," said Anne. "Even with the hard-working technicians we've got following orangutans in the forest, it's a logistic nightmare to track all of them. In fact, it's virtually impossible. We just do not have the personnel, the money or the know-how to monitor several hundred released orangutans. We can only hope that at least some of them succeed in establishing independent lives."

"But what about the other ones?" said Shane. "The ones you don't know about."

"Duh," said Alice, who understood the implication of Anne's words.

"What? You mean... they've died?" said Shane.

"We have to consider that as a possibility," said Anne. "Sometimes death occurs despite our good intentions."

"What do you mean?" asked Alice.

"It's difficult to know what to look for in evaluating the health of a free-living orangutan. Sometimes the clues can be pretty subtle, like dull hair, excessive weight loss, or listlessness. Unless you see an orangutan regularly, changes can be hard to detect, even for experts. Sometimes the technicians who monitor the orangutans regularly don't notice the problem or if they do notice, they don't report it. They hope the problem will cure itself, and sometimes it does."

"So, how do the technicians know what to look for?" asked Alice. "Is there an orangutan school they go to?"

Anne laughed. "I wish there was, but there's not. The closest we come to Orangutan U. is to hold classes at the rehab center. In the forest, technicians accompany researchers on follows, and that's another way they learn to be good observers. If they see an orangutan with dull hair, or one with ribs sticking out, or one that spends a lot of time on the ground, they'll know those signs may be indicators of poor health. And we hope they'll report it to one of the vets so the orangutan can be treated," said Anne.

"You hope?" said Shane. "Why wouldn't they report it?"

"It's a cultural thing," said Anne. "Indonesians don't like to be the bearers of bad news, so problems are sometimes ignored. Last year there was a French graduate student who was working in the forest studying orangutan nests. Miss Nest, we called her. Miss Nest noticed that one rehabbed orangutan was spending a lot of time on the ground, and it looked to her like it might have parasites."

"Parasites?" said Shane. "What kind of parasites would they be?"

"They would be microscopic organisms that take up residence in the orangutan's digestive tract and rob him of the nutrients he should get from food," Anne explained. "Anyway, Miss Nest reported this behavior and her hunch to one of the technicians, but he couldn't recognize the problem, so it was ignored. When I arrived, I looked at the orangutan along with Miss Nest and all the technicians, and we immediately radioed the head of the center and had the orangutan taken to the clinic."

"So, he was okay?" asked Shane.

Anne sighed. "He died the next day."

"That's so sad," said Alice, shaking her head.

"Dang," said Shane. "That shouldn't have happened."

"A lot of things shouldn't happen, but they do," said Anne. "The little guy's death might have been prevented if all of our forest technicians knew how to recognize the danger signs earlier, and knew what needed serious attention."

"Can't they be trained better?"

"Training is a problem," said Anne, with a shrug. "A lot of the technicians are conscientious like Iyan, but to some of them, watching after orangutans is just a job. When there's no one around to supervise them, they have nothing to rely on but their own understanding and their own perspective. They may not always take into account that they are dealing with the survival of a species here. Either that or they just don't care, the same way many North Americans wouldn't care if they lost a few bears from their favorite campground."

"Man, don't tell me about bears," said Shane. "Last summer I was camping up in the Sierra with a couple of buddies and the first night out we hoisted our backpacks up a tree, but that didn't stop this one particular black bear. The sucker ripped off all our beef jerky. It sure wouldn't bother me if that guy took a permanent hike."

"Stole your jerky?" said Alice. "All those preservatives probably made him sick."

"Do you think you could tell a sick bear if you saw one?" asked Anne.

"I don't know," said Alice with a shrug. "Probably not."

"Not unless he was like barfing or something," said Shane.

"Sometimes it's pretty hard to tell if an animal is sick," said Anne. "So we can't really blame the technicians for not noticing something that's barely noticeable in the first place."

"So, how would a Halfway Forest help?" asked Alice.

Anne cheered up a bit when the conversation turned from problem to solution. "The rehab center's been given access to ten hectares of prime forest. It's full of wild fruit trees, perfect orangutan habitat."

"Whose land is it?"

"It belongs to the national oil company, Pertamina."

"They're willing to sell it?"

"Better than that," said Anne. "They're willing to let us use it free of charge for ten years. All we have to do is put a wall around it."

"A wall?" said Alice. "How much will that cost?"

"About fifty thousand U.S. dollars," said Anne.

Shane let out a low whistle. "Dang, that's a good chunk of change. Where's it going to come from?"

"We don't really know," said Anne. "But the important thing is that we have the land. We've got a site with lots of trees that's close to the rehab center. Orangutans can work on their survival skills there under supervision. That way we'll know whether or not they have learned the necessary survival skills before they are released into the unsupervised forest. We're even toying with the possibility of orangutan nannies, you know, older females with forest experience who can show the youngsters how to build nests, or how to get food from a bandang tree, or peel bark from an acacia."

"Sort of like camp counselors," said Shane.

"Saving a species from extinction sure is a lot of hard work," said Alice.

"Yeah," Shane chimed in. "And there's no guarantees."

"But we have to try," said Anne. "Sometimes, with a little luck, our methods work. Just look at Uce, here. But sometimes they fail. We have to learn from our failures. We hope the Halfway Forest will provide a huge piece of the rehabilitation puzzle."

"I'm trying to understand the whole orangutan problem," said Alice, drawing a circle in the ground with a stick and dividing it into three parts. "From what we've learned just hanging out with you, it seems that the reason orangutans are in so much trouble is because of poaching and loss of habitat, and because they don't have many babies."

"In a nutshell," said Anne. "Orangutans are in trouble wherever they exist on Borneo and Sumatra. They have lots of enemies: poachers who supply babies to the illegal pet market, timber companies and loggers whose logging practices and illegal lumber harvests leave orangutans without food and shelter. And, of course, all this is compounded by their own slow reproductive rate. But there's one more very important part of the equation to consider if the orangutans are going to be saved: education. We've got to educate people about why orangutans are important to the health of the forest. The subsistence farmers who grow just enough bananas and vegetables to feed their families are just as likely as not to shoot or hack to death an orangutan that comes into their garden."

"How's an orangutan supposed to know that the bananas he finds growing in some farmer's garden are not meant for him?" said Shane. "Especially if he's been fed bananas in the rehab center."

"An orangutan can't know," said Anne, "so the answer lies in educating the farmer. But the farmer is poor, and can barely provide food for his children. What reason can we give him not to kill an orangutan that is raiding his garden and eating food meant to feed his family? Do you think he cares that the orangutan is facing extinction?"

"I guess not," said Shane. "He'd probably be happy about it."

"Do you think he would ever put an orangutan's survival ahead of his family's?" asked Anne.

"No way," said Shane.

"If the farmer is living day-to-day," said Alice, "he's not going to understand much about forest diversity, and even if he did, he's not going to care when his own family's survival is at stake."

"But if the orangutans, and all the parts of the ecosystem connected to the orangutans, are going to survive, the people who live on this island and on Sumatra have to understand why they are important. And that requires education, and education in a country as poor as this one is a luxury available only to the rich. The education of human beings—who are, after all, the dominant species on the planet—is the number one priority," said Anne. "If the orangutan is going to survive, we have to change the way people think."

"Geez," said Alice. "That's not going to be easy."

"It sure isn't," agreed Shane.

"And what do you tell the local poacher who gets more money for one baby orangutan than he can earn in a year working on an oil palm plantation? What incentive does he have to stop poaching?"

"Jail?" said Shane.

"Poaching is against the law," said Alice, as if that alone should make a difference.

"Laws are only as good as their enforcement," said Anne. "The local poacher and the smuggler both know that the odds of getting caught are slim to none. To the poacher, looking helplessly at his starving kids in their ragged clothes and knowing their lack of future, the reward is well worth the risk. Do you know how many orangutans die for every baby that reaches the black market?"

"Two?" guessed Alice.

"I have no clue," said Shane.

"Four or five, at least," said Anne. "The mother is always killed. And many of the babies die of shock or malnutrition before they reach the marketplace. The cruel conditions these babies suffer on their way to becoming someone's cherished pet, or child substitute, would break your heart."

"Child substitute?" said Shane.

"Like Jude," whispered Alice.

"Some people who cannot have children of their own keep an orangutan as a sort of surrogate child," said Anne. "Of course when the orangutan turns seven or eight and starts going through all kinds of hormonal changes, their owners no longer want them. We get lots of those cases at the center."

"So what is the answer, Anne? There must be something that can be done," said Alice.

"The orangutan survival problem is a puzzle," said Anne. "There are just a handful of people working on the puzzle, and each is contributing a small piece. Unfortunately, the clock is ticking and the problem is growing much faster than solutions can be discovered and implemented. Worldwide, there are really very few people working to save the orangutans. We need a bigger army."

"What about kids like Alice and me?" said Shane. "We're a big army. The kids at the international school did something."

"But what can we do?" asked Alice.

"Well, let's all give that a little thought this afternoon, and maybe we can come up with some ideas," said Anne.

Uce, who had been nursing her baby during Anne's and the children's conversation, now turned and crabbed into the forest with her infant's arms wrapped around her neck.

"Good-bye, Uce," called Anne. "God, I hope she'll be all right. I worry about her and that baby."

"You mean because of poachers?" asked Alice, and Anne nodded solemnly.

"Do you hear something?" said Shane.

"Nope, just the bugs," said Alice.

"What do you hear, Shane?" asked Anne.

"Something's crashing through the woods," said Shane. "But it's pretty far away."

"Maybe it's Nik," Alice said.

"Nik would likely be in the canopy," said Anne.

"I don't know," said Shane. "Maybe I'm hearing things."

And then a voice, a deep baritone, wafted through the forest, "Halloooooo, Anne!"

Anne turned in the direction of the voice. "It's Willie."

The Confiscation

Wait a minute, you might be saying to yourself right about now. Who is Willie again? His full name is Willie Smits, and he is a Dutch forester and microbiologist. It was he who rescued Uce, and he is still rescuing orangutans. Right now he is making his way along the trail through the forest toward Camp Djamaludin. Before we go on with today's story, let's find out what Willie did yesterday. —Alice's dad

Yesterday, at about the time Alice and Shane were setting Yayat free, Willie and an orangutan confiscation team were village-hopping their way up the Mahakam river into the remote, primitive heart of Borneo. They traveled, in the muggy heat of midday, in a yellow speedboat. With its fiberglass hull bleached and faded from years of tropical sun, it looked a bit like the pale, dry corpse of a yellowjacket found on a windowsill. The runabout's Naughahyde seats were torn, and the foam stuffing bulged from their ripped edges. None of the gauges on the boat's instrument panel functioned, not even the gas gauge. The out-of-tune, forty-five-horse-power outboard engine mounted on the boat's transom sputtered and coughed, rather than purred. But it generated enough power so that the hull bounced along, slapping the waves and causing the pair of large, empty aluminum cages in the back seat to clang together like empty trash cans.

Accompanying Willie on this particular confiscation mission were Dr. Amir, the veterinarian in charge of the medical clinic at the rehabilitation center, and Ibu Nita, the woman responsible for the operational management of the center. Also present in the speedboat was a local law enforcement officer, uncomfortable in his uniform and with the burden of power that compelled him to place under arrest poachers and smugglers careless enough to be caught with an orangutan.

The Mahakam, as it meandered through the rain forest on its serpentine journey from the highland forest to the sea, was the color of a brown paper bag. Its water was clouded with silt and mud released by upstream clear-cuts and recent fires. Carried in its current was much debris—logs, floating islands of trees, and an occasional domestic animal such as a pig, belly up, its legs stiff, hooves pointing accusingly at the sullen sky.

Willie was perched on the back of the runabout's front seat, his hands on the wheel and his sandal-clad feet on the ripped cushion. His wavy brown hair danced over his collar like strands of kelp in an underwater garden. From the boat he could see a fringe of forest leaning over the river's banks like a thirsty dog over its water dish. Not so long ago, during past trips up the Mahakam, Willie had spotted numerous proboscis monkeys, and many pairs of rhinoceros hornbills on the wing, noisily shredding the damp air with broad strokes of their powerful wings as they followed the graceful bends of the river. Now Willie squinted at the brushed aluminum sky, hazy and bright, that seemed to have suffocated the life out of the river. There was no sound, no whirring of insects nor bubbling gibbon calls, no cackling hornbills; no signs of wildlife whatsoever. An unnatural stillness prevailed. Suddenly he heard a resonant thud, like the hollow beat of a tribal drum, as the thin hull struck a log. The sound echoed in Willie's mind and brought him back into the present.

An hour later, Willie guided the boat to a dilapidated pier that marked the location of Long Bau, a Dayak village of several hundred inhabitants. A few women and children were gathered on the dock to wash clothes and exchange the news of the day. Willie cut the engine and let the boat drift toward the dock. As Dr. Amir tied the boat up, Willie asked the women on the pier if they knew of anyone who had an orangutan. The women and children, choreographed to deny, shook their heads in unison: no, they knew of no one who had an orangutan.

Then a thin man wearing ragged shorts and a stained T-shirt stepped forward and said, "I may know of someone who has one."

"Will you take me to them?" asked Willie, unable to avert his eyes from the mango-sized tumor growing on the side of the man's head.

"Perhaps I might be persuaded to act as your guide," said the man coyly.

"Yes," said Willie, understanding that the man was asking for payment to show him to the house where an orangutan might or might not be held captive. To Ibu Nita, Dr. Amir and the policeman, Willie said, "Wait here while I check this out."

As the old man and Willie walked through the dusty streets in the blazing sun, Willie felt the heat on his back. Two men sat in the shade of a fig tree at the side of the road, cutting up bark whose fumes, when burned, repelled mosquitoes. They nodded indifferently as Willie and the old man walked purposefully past. Ahead of them a lone stork with a bald pink head and bright red wattle wandered unmolested through the deserted streets like a visitor from another planet. The houses were modest, unpainted structures, some with thatched roofs and some with tin. They were all built on stilts to deter vermin and were without doors or windows. The old man stopped at a house at the edge of the village. "In there," he said, with a casual wave of his hand. "The woman has a baby orangutan. I have seen it." Trusting that the old man was telling the truth, Willie reached into his pocket for a wad of bills and peeled off a twenty thousand rupiah note, equal to about two U.S. dollars. The old man acknowledged the money gratefully before shuffling off.

Willie knocked at the door, and a woman emerged from the shadows. Like everyone in the village, she had the gaunt, hollow look of the malnourished. Her pierced earlobes were stretched and distorted; she had many dark bruise-like tattoos, and smoked a thick, aromatic cigarette. Between her puffs of smoke Willie saw that her teeth were stained blood-red from chewing betel nuts.

"Are you keeping an orangutan here?" Willies asked in fluent Indonesian.

"Do you want to buy it?" said the woman, mistaking Willie for a smuggler.

"Are you aware that it is illegal to keep an orangutan?"

The woman eyed him cautiously and shrugged.

"I am here as a representative of the Indonesian government to confiscate the orangutan you are keeping. May I see it, please?"

The woman took a deep drag from her cigarette and with a long sigh, gave up. "My husband will be angry," she said.

"It is my job to take the orangutan from you," said Willie.

With her head, the woman gestured for Willie to follow. She led him through the house, out the back door, across a narrow catwalk littered on either side with the debris of everyday life, to a dark toilet where a small wooden crate sat on the damp floor. Two round brown eyes surrounded by a disc of pink skin peered out from between the slats.

"How long have you had this infant?" asked Willie, squatting for a closer look, careful not to soil his trousers on the filthy wooden floor.

"Two months, maybe three."

"Have you ever let him out of this crate?"

The woman shook her head and said, no, she hadn't, but maybe her husband had. She didn't know. Willie pulled the top board off the crate and an emaciated male infant leaped out and, despite its weak condition, climbed quickly up Willie's torso and threw his arms around his neck. His dull red hair was matted with his own excrement. The stench was overwhelming. When Willie pinched the orangutan's loose skin, it did not return to its original shape, a symptom of dehydration. At the bottom of the cage, the excrement was fifteen centimeters deep.

"Why do you keep this baby?" asked Willie.

The woman shrugged indifferently. "For a pet," she said. Then she added, "We have no children."

"A pet?" said Willie suspiciously. "Not to sell?" He wanted to ask the woman if this is how she would treat the child she did not have, but held his tongue.

"No," the woman said. "Not to sell."

"What pleasure can there be in keeping a baby orangutan in a crate in your dark toilet?"

"It is my husband's wish," she said.

"Where is your husband?"

"He is not here."

"Where did he get this baby?"

"He did not say."

Willie told the woman to expect a visit from the local police and was walking toward the door when his eyes were drawn to an orangutan skull hanging on the wall. The skull was carved with traditional Dayak motifs, but the carving looked fresh, as if the linear designs had recently been scratched into the bone. Willie pointed to the skull and looked at the woman imploringly. She nodded toward the infant clinging to Willie's neck. "Mama," she said simply.

"I thought you didn't know where the infant came from," said Willie.

"The mother was in our garden, eating our food," the woman confessed. "What can we do? We are poor and do not have enough to eat. We cannot be expected to share what little food we have with orangutans."

"What did you do with the mother's body?" asked Willie.

"We ate it," said the woman, as the long ash from her cigarette floated to the floor.

A s Willie walked back toward the boat, he wore the infant orangutan like a red necklace. Behind him he heard someone call, "Mister, mister." He turned to see a man hurrying to catch him. The man was out of breath when he reached Willie.

"I want to be paid for the baby," he told Willie, gruffly.

"No," said Willie. "We do not pay anything to people who poach orangutans."

"But why not?" the man demanded. "All the time foreigners come into the village and pay two hundred thousand rupiahs for a baby. How can that be wrong?"

"It is wrong because it is against the law," said Willie, eyeing the crowd that had started to gather.

"Well, will you give us money for food?" said the man. "I was counting on selling the baby to buy food for my family. It hasn't rained, and our rice crop has failed two years in a row."

At this point the village head stepped out of the crowd and stood next to the poacher. A thin man with sunken cheeks, he was dressed in torn shorts and a soiled New York Knicks T-shirt. Willie thought for a minute, and surveyed the small crowd. He reached into his pocket and gave the village head a few hundred thousand rupiahs. "I want you to understand that this money is for food for your village. I am not giving you this money for the baby orangutan. I am giving this money to the village because I understand your village has suffered from the drought and fires and there is not enough to eat." The village head nodded gratefully and the villagers murmured approvingly. "This money is not payment for the orangutan," Willie said again. "No one will be compensated for poaching an orangutan. Is that understood?" The village head nodded in agreement, as did the villagers.

It was late afternoon when Willie, with the baby orangutan still clinging to his shoulder, guided the boat up a tributary of the Mahakam toward the village of Jak Luay, where they had heard of another orangutan in need of rescue. The man who was keeping this orangutan was called Paulus, and his house sat on stilts over the river. Once again, they found a young orangutan. This one was a female about four years old and she was also imprisoned in a small crate in a dark and dank toilet. The small female displayed the heartbreaking symptoms of stress; her fingers were bloody stumps that she had gnawed off. There was a gaping wound in the lower part of her abdomen from which a putrid stench emanated; Willie guessed that it might have been caused by a bullet or a spear. A scar ringed her neck, and large patches of skin were missing from her hands and feet. Dr. Amir gave her an injection of tranquilizers. Paulus, who was employed at a nearby oil palm plantation, told Willie he caught this orangutan alone without its mother in his cornfield.

"Are you sure you did not kill her mother?" Willie asked bluntly.

"I didn't," said Paulus.

"Where did the wounds come from?"

"She had the wounds when I captured her. Maybe she was injured by another hunter."

"Another hunter?" said Willie. "Do you hunt orangutans?"

"I used to hunt them, but I don't anymore."

"Why not?" asked Willie. He did not believe Paulus.

"Two years ago I spot a mother with her baby up a tree," said Paulus. "I have my rifle. I take aim and I shoot the mother, but she does not fall. She climbs down the tree very slowly and there is a smear of blood on the bark where her body has pressed against the tree. When she reaches the bottom of the tree she crawls over to me and looks up into my eyes. Then she lays her baby at my feet, and she dies."

CHAPTER 13

The Wall

A s Alice used her shirttail to dab at the tears that suddenly sprung to her eyes, Shane cleared his throat then asked Willie, "Did all that stuff really happen?"

"I'm afraid so," said Willie, blowing on his tea to cool it before taking a sip. "That and more, much more. Always it's the same story—a starving female orangutan with a baby to care for comes into the garden looking for food. She's invariably spotted by the farmer and killed. The baby is snatched and sold to a pet trader. It's the same old story, and it happens over and over again."

"But why?" said Alice, using her fork to probe her noodles. She had suddenly lost her appetite. "Why does it have to keep happening over and over? Why can't it stop?"

"Indonesia is a poor country," said Willie with a shrug, not of indifference, but of the knowledge that this was just the way things were in this part of the world. "Crimes against nature occur frequently in poor countries. The poverty makes it happen. It's not that people don't care about the orangutan. If anyone has an appreciation of the forest and its inhabitants, it's the people whose lives depend upon its bounty for their livelihood. But like the orangutan, they are starving. The drought has caused their rice crops to fail two years running. They've stood by helplessly and watched as their forest is first logged, then burned and then replaced by palm oil and rubber tree plantations that benefit them very little."

"But what about the jobs?" asked Shane. "Don't all those new plantations mean work for the people who live in the forest?"

"Oh, some of them have low-paying jobs logging, or harvesting the oil palms or rubber, but it means abandoning a way of life and a culture that have been established for hundreds of years. The companies that own the land and make policy don't really care much about the people they hire. If a tree falls on a logger and kills him, they just hire another logger. There's no insurance, no pensions. The supply of workers is endless. They're just a commodity to the plantation owners, like a tractor or a chainsaw."

"Sounds like what happened in the United States a hundred years or so ago," said Alice. "And that started the Civil War."

"There's a lot of unrest throughout Indonesia. The social and economic situation can easily ignite a war, and it has. That's what happens when people are miserable and without hope and feel their government is indifferent to their needs. They want change, and they want it now. They're tired of waiting, and they're tired of promises that are never kept," said Willie. "Can you understand now why poaching orangutans is so attractive to the villagers? It's next to impossible to teach conservation to people who do not have enough to eat and who, out of desperation, will kill and eat the very animal we are trying to save."

"Educating them is no easy task," added Anne.

"Education, at least education about orangutans, has very little relevance to people whose main focus in life is to provide for their families," agreed Willie.

"But orangutans are almost… people," said Alice, as if that alone should exempt them from human avarice.

"Yes, but look what people do to one another," said Anne. "Look what has happened in East Timor—thousands of people died because they dared to express their opinion."

"Dang," said Shane, staring into his bowl of noodles and shaking his head. "This is depressing."

"But there's a bit of good news in the midst of all this doom and gloom,

Willie," said Anne. "We saw Uce this afternoon, and she has a baby!"

"A baby!" says Willie, his brown eyes twinkling and his face breaking into a broad grin. "That's fantastic! We haven't seen Uce in several years."

"I was beginning to wonder if she had left the forest, or if she was even still alive," said Anne. "And this afternoon there she was. I took a photograph of her and her baby."

"Can you e-mail me a copy?" said Willie. "Who knows when we'll see her again."

"Or if we'll see her again," said Anne gloomily. "Thinking of her out there in the woods with a baby makes me afraid for her—she's so vulnerable."

"Poachers," said Shane.

Willie and Anne both shook their heads. "If they find her, yes. We can only hope she has enough sense to hide when she hears strangers in the woods," said Willie. Trying to be optimistic about this miracle birth that had taken place against all odds he added, "Uce's baby proves that a captive orangutan that has been returned to the forest can procreate."

"But if Uce's in danger..." said Alice.

"This is a protected forest," said Willie with a sigh, knowing that even though the forest was protected, it was not protected well enough.

"Yes," said Anne, "but protection without proper enforcement is no protection at all."

"It's too bad the forest isn't fenced," said Shane offhandedly. "It needs a wall around it like your Halfway Forest."

"Yes," said Willie, "we've thought of that. A wall, or at least a fence, would offer some deterrent to poachers."

"How big is this forest?" said Alice.

"It used to be about 10,000 hectares," said Anne. "But now the good forest has been reduced to about 3,500 hectares. It's the last bit of primary forest left in this area, and it's the main watershed for Balikpapan."

"It shrank?" asked Shane. "How did it shrink?"

"Encroachment and fires," said Willie. "Fires in 1998 wiped out about 3,500 hectares. Subsistence farmers have claimed the rest. Once the farmers are entrenched, it's very hard to get them to move."

"But it's not their land," said Alice. "That kind of stuff wouldn't happen in the States."

"Probably not today, but squatting used to be common in the States and it's still a legitimate way to lay claim to land in many parts of the world," said Anne, running her fingers through her dense tangle of curls. "And Borneo's the Wild West of Indonesia. It's the country's biggest island, and its size makes it very difficult to patrol. The people are very family-oriented. When someone from East Kalimantan tells a relative from Sulawesi how much opportunity there is here they pack their few possessions, hop a boat and sail over. Before you know it they've cleared a plot of land, put up a shack and planted a garden, which of course acts like a magnet for the orangutans. If the local police or forestry officials pay them a visit and tell them they are living on land that is protected, they just shrug and say, 'Oh? Where is the boundary?' "

"I like Shane's idea of building a wall around the forest," said Alice. "That way there would be a boundary."

"Yes," said Anne. "A line of demarcation would be impossible to ignore."

"But why can't a wall be built?" said Shane.

"Because building a wall would cost a lot of money," said Willie. "And there is no money. A fence would be less expensive and would at least provide that line of demarcation."

"How much would a fence cost?" asked Alice.

"Maybe fifty or a hundred thousand dollars," said Willie, "depending on what kind is built." He shook his head. "With all the other problems in Indonesia, and the constant flow of new orangutans coming to the rehab center each week, there is just no money left to build a fence."

"Fifty thousand dollars doesn't seem like so much," said Alice. "It costs that much to remodel a kitchen back home."

"Shoot," said Shane. "I know people who paid more for their pickup trucks than that."

"Maybe we could raise money if we put a little book or something together that explains why the orangutans need help," said Alice.

"Yeah," said Shane. "I've been taking a lot of photos of the orangutans I've seen. Maybe we could use some of those."

"There must be something we can do to get the word out," said Alice.

"I've got lots of photos, too," said Anne.

"Maybe we could make a book out of them," said Alice.

"Yeah, like a postcard book," said Shane, grinning now as the idea took shape in his mind. "That'd be cool."

"A postcard book," said Willie. "I like that idea."

"Yeah, and kids could sell the books to people and all the money could go toward building the fence," said Alice.

"A postcard book is an interesting concept," said Anne. "People could either keep it together like a book, or tear the cards out and send them to their friends. That way the orangutan message would reach new people."

"It could work," said Willie, nodding his head with approval. "You kids really think you can put something like this together?"

"Piece of cake," said Shane confidently. "I can do it on my computer."

"You know," said Alice, "if we raised enough money we could eventually get a wall built around the whole forest, and that would be much better protection than a fence. Never underestimate the power of kids," she added, winding noodles around her fork. "We're all just bricks in the wall, to quote Pink Floyd, but together we can accomplish a lot."

"Pink Floyd?" said Anne, her eyebrows arching dubiously above her glasses. "Isn't that the song that starts off with 'We don't need no education?'"

"Yeah," said Alice, "but that's not true, everybody needs education. I think that part of the song was just, you know, rock and roll."

"Alice is right, we're all just bricks," said Shane. "And by ourselves that's all we are. But, you know what? If we join together, we can build a wall and, just maybe, our wall can change the world."

"Or at least create a safe haven for orangutans until the world does change," said Anne wistfully.

CHAPTER 14

The Rehab Center

Having come this far, you've read several mentions of orangutans having "rehab" at "the center." The rehabilitation center is a real place, almost too real. At this point in our story I thought it would be appropriate to invite you to join Alice and Shane on a tour of the center, so that you can visualize it yourself and get a feeling for what goes on there. —Alice's dad

The origins of the Wanariset Orangutan Reintroduction Center speak clearly of the power children have to change their world. It was in 1991 that Willie Smits was offered a baby orangutan in an open market in the bustling Indonesian oil metropolis of Balikpapan. Willie took the female orangutan baby home where he and his sons, students at the Pasir Ridge International School in Balikpapan, named her Uce and nursed her back to health. Soon another orphaned baby orangutan in crisis was brought to Willie, then another. The students at Pasir Ridge recognized the orangutan problem and chose to became part of its solution, rather than stand hopelessly and ineffectually on the perimeter of the situation, waiting for someone else to step forward and take action.

Hopeful? Or hopeless? It was hard to tell with this guy. S.B.

The students pooled their energies and solicited the support of their parents, many of whom were employees of offshore companies with holdings and interests in Indonesia. Their work led to the establishment of a rehabilitation center in East Kalimantan, which is on the outskirts of Balikpapan. Such were the humble beginnings of the Wanariset Orangutan Reintroduction Center and its support group, the Balikpapan Orangutan Society.

Orphaned, displaced, confiscated and surrendered orangutans can now be brought to Wanariset for rehabilitation. If an orangutan's rehabilitation process is successful, it is then scheduled for "reintroduction," that is, for release into a remote, protected forest of good orangutan habitat.

Before we begin our tour, I must warn you, just as I was warned when I first arrived. Try not to be too shocked or dismayed by the pictures you will see here and the images that will soon be drawn in your mind's eye. Conditions at Wanariset are improving rapidly, but it is still a refugee camp and there are many more orangutans here than there is space to accommodate them properly.

The clusters of cages that house the sick, injured and displaced orangutans are arranged on a steep hillside and accessible by long flights of cement stairs

1500 kilos is a big bunch of bananas. S.B.

that wind through the compound. Some of the stairs have ramps running down their centers, making smooth paths that wheelbarrow wheels can roll over so food can be delivered to the orangutans without being bruised. Can you imagine how many wheelbarrow trips up and down the stairs it takes to deliver 1500 kilos of bananas to nearly 300 hungry orangutans? Did someone mention that conservation is hard work? It is some of the hardest, and most important, work in the world and by their very nature, conservationists are optimists. They don't give up, even in the face of overwhelming odds, because they can't give up.

Here we are on the observation deck, and the view from here is all that most Wanariset visitors are permitted. A steady stream of visitors past the cages would benefit neither the rescued orangutans living here nor their rehabilitation process. Wanariset is not an orangutan zoo but rather a place where the serious work of saving orangutans from extinction is an ongoing process. See that adult male, holding onto the bars in that white tiled cage that Unocal has sponsored? He sits there like that all day, every day, like some sort of orangutan figurine. He never moves. I wonder what he thinks about all day? What memories does he hold in his mind?

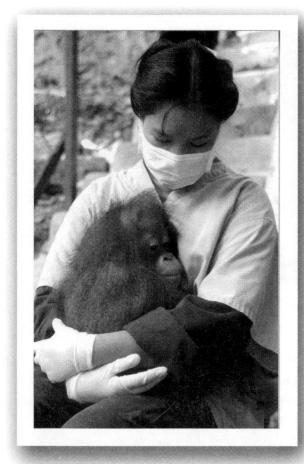

This girl lives in a village near the rehab center.
She cuddles orphans six hours a day. S.B.

Since we're not most visitors, and this tour is taking place in our imaginations, follow me through this iron gate that has been left unlocked for our benefit. Watch your step; these stairs are slippery. Here we are at the first landing. The white building on our left is the clinic where sick orangutans are treated by the team of veterinarians and paramedics who live at the center and staff the clinic twenty-four hours a day, seven days a week, every day of the year. Right over here, across from the clinic, we see a small glass building that looks like a child's playhouse. If we peek through the paint-splattered panes we can see half a dozen orphans looking back at us at with uncomprehending eyes. Maybe they think we can restore order to their lives. Look at that pair of infants cuddling each other. Baby orangutans thrive on the constant physical contact they once received from their mothers; that's why these two are clinging to each other. But it looks as if these guys are excluding that other little fellow who wants to be part of the cuddle puddle, too. Poor little guy, his buddies don't know there's enough love to go around. See that young woman sitting on that bench over there cuddling an infant? She lives in a nearby village and her job is to hold and bestow affection

If there's anything cuter than a baby orangutan, I sure don't know what it is. Of course, being so cute is one of their problems. S.B.

on baby orangutans. A professional cuddler, that's what she is.

While Shane is busy photographing the nursery, let's continue our tour.

Directly across the path from the infants, next to the clinic, is the quarantine cage. This is where juveniles must be kept if they are suspected carriers of hepatitis B or tuberculosis. Now you might wonder, as I did, how an orangutan can catch hepatitis B and tuberculosis, human diseases. Orangutans share 97% of their DNA with their human kin and they catch some of the same diseases. Many of the orangutans in this cage have come from human households where they have been exposed to their diseases.

Let's head down the stairs. These two rows of little cages you see here are pretty grim. I think they were some of the original ones and were built a long time ago. I hope so anyway. Let's wait a minute; Shane wants to take another photograph. The way the orangutans' sad, peach-colored faces emerge from the darkness of these small cages reminds me of a Rembrandt painting. (Like Willie Smits, Rembrandt was a passionate Dutchman.)

Over here, past the tree planted to commemorate a visit from Queen Beatrice

One of the technicians at the rehab center
offers a helping hand. S.B.

of the Netherlands, is a large socialization cage. As you can see, it's made of strong, three-quarter-inch iron bars welded together. As you know, even juvenile and subadult orangutans are strong; an adult male can have eight times the strength of a typical man. Here comes a technician to give them their daily dose of medicine from a spoon. Look at the way the orangutans line up inside their cage with their long gray fingers wrapped around the bars. Look how they pucker their lips to receive the medication. They must like the taste of it.

This cage over here holds mothers with babies in their own individual cells. The goal is to have them feel as secure as possible. This sad-eyed female and her infant are victims of the fires that, in 1997 and 1998, collectively burned a hole in Borneo the size of Northern Ireland. How big is that, you ask? Well, look on a globe. Trace the shape of Northern Ireland on a piece of paper, then hold the paper over the island of Borneo. That's how much rain forest habitat has been lost to fires. Look at that mother's stare. It's the only defense she has left to protect her baby.

The large adult over here with the impressive cheekpads is Romeo. Normally

Until the recent fires, this mother and her baby lived in the forest.
Now they live in a white tiled cage. Who knows for how long? S.B.

males don't develop cheekpads until they are fourteen or fifteen years of age, but life in captivity has accelerated Romeo's maturing process. Look at how powerfully he is built, and imagine the strength he must have in his hands. You can see just by looking into his eyes how intelligent he is. What's that gold thing in his mouth? It looks like part of a padlock. Hey, Shane, that'd be a good photograph, very metaphoric. Romeo is one of the Taiwan Ten. Alice and Shane, you'll remember Nik's telling you about them. They were rescued in 1992 in an effort to interrupt the illegal orangutan trade to Taiwan. Because no one could figure out what else to do with them, they were flown back to Borneo. Romeo has been here since he was five years old, a juvenile. Romeo's burden is that every time he is tested for hepatitis B, the results are positive, so he is ineligible for release. Even if he could be released, he's probably too old to learn how to survive on his own in the forest. Unlike Nik, Romeo will never build a nest high in the forest canopy and enjoy a tropical sunrise. And unlike Bento, he'll never know the sweet taste of umbut. His view of life will be forever dissected by vertical iron bars, like an innocent man mistakenly condemned to a life sentence

I spent a lot of time looking at Romeo looking back at me. I don't know... it felt like there was something between us besides just the bars. S.B.

by a system that has failed him.

Well, there you have it, end of tour. These refugees are not a pretty sight, are they? Wanariset is not a perfect place, but it's the only place these orangutans have. The people who work here, the vets, the technicians, the cooks, the researchers, the cuddlers, the drivers who make long journeys to the release forests over dangerous roads, are all part of a team doing the best job they can to teach orangutans the skills they will need if they are to live independent lives in the forest.

It's important to remember that each of these orangutans is here because at some point during the course of their lives they were unlucky enough to cross paths with human civilization. Some are here because their mothers have been murdered, which, as you know by now, is the only way an infant can be obtained for the illegal pet trade. Some are here because their rain forest has been razed, slashed and burned to create space for oil palm and rubber tree plantations, or rice paddies and small subsistence farms. Some are here because they have been

This guy seems to be saying, "Hey, what happened? Let me out of here." S.B.

confiscated from people who wanted to own an orangutan as a pet. They are here because citizens who have learned, too late, that orangutans do not make good pets have surrendered them. They are here because they have contracted human diseases. They are all here to await uncertain fates, to stare into the black hole of extinction. Some of them, like Romeo, have no hope of release. For others the future is brighter and looms like a question mark. But every one of these orangutans is here at Wanariset because of the unconscionable avarice, cruelty and ignorance of human beings.

We should also remember that these orangutans are also here because a few human beings care about them.

We're walking up past the infants' cage again and, look at that. The little orangutan that was being excluded by two of his mates is now clinging to them in a cozy threesome.

Hey, don't tell me there's no hope at all.

The Old Man
of the Forest

S hane rolled out from beneath the mosquito netting before dawn and pulled on his boots. He grabbed his backpack from the nail by the door, hoisted it over his shoulder, and walked out into the cool morning mist. His goal this morning was to take a photograph of the sunlight as it streamed through the trees and foliage not far from camp. The way the sun's rays broke through the canopy and wrapped the dangling lianas, lichen-splotched trunks and broad green leaves in a film of translucent yellow light screamed (in a reverently quiet way, of course) "rain forest" more than any other image Shane could imagine. And what about the creatures that inhabited the rain forest? Wouldn't a photograph of the animal residents be more representative of this well populated rain forest? Maybe, and then again, maybe not. Shane's grandfather had told him how difficult it would be to photograph wild animals, how elusive and shy they were. But even though there were no wild animals posing for his photograph, Shane satisfied himself with the idea that they were really there, you just couldn't see them. Who knew how many cicadas, beetles, frogs, wild pigs, civets, pythons, flying foxes, proboscis monkeys, tarsiers or, for that matter, orangutans were hiding in plain sight? Shane had a feeling that this was the only time he would be in this particular place, and he wanted to make a photograph that would capture its essence and remind him what a beautiful and unique part of the world Borneo was turning out to be.

Shane steadied his camera against the trunk of a tree, squinted into the viewfinder, and waited patiently for the light to stream through the mist that was trapped high in the canopy. Ah, here it came…long, buttery spikes, perfect blades of translucent yellow light, just as he had hoped. The moment had arrived. Gently, so as not to move the camera, he depressed the shutter. Ka-lop it went as the mirror inside flipped up to expose the film. A quarter of a second, he thought, was really too slow to hold steady without a tripod, at least with this particular lens. He hoped the tree trunk would give his camera the support it needed for a sharp photograph. But to be on the safe side, he decided to expose one more frame, this time opening the lens to a wider aperture and exposing the film for an eighth of a second. This faster shutter speed would give him a better chance at a sharp photograph, though the wider aperture would sacrifice some depth of focus. Once again he peered into the viewfinder and held his breath as he prepared to depress the shutter. Then he saw movement in the upper part of the frame. What the heck is that? he thought, a bird? He watched as a foot and then an entire leg descended slowly into the frame. The hairy edges of the leg, backlit by the morning sun, seemed to be on fire. He peered over the camera. It was Gomez, climbing down the tree to star in his photograph. Shane peered into the viewfinder again and turned the ring on the lens to snap the scene into focus. When Gomez's little egg-shaped body was all the way in the frame, Shane held his breath and pressed the shutter button. His heart pulsed within his chest as he felt, for the first time, the thrill all photographers feel when they capture a once-in-a-lifetime image on film. To a photographer, whether a seasoned pro or a novice like Shane, nothing is quite as satisfying as knowing his vision and photographic skills have merged in the right place at the right time. "I must be living right," Shane whispered to himself. "Ibu Anne said Borneo had a lot to teach me, and dang if I'm not learning it."

When Gomez reached the forest floor, he crabbed over to Shane, looked up at him with his innocent brown marble eyes and said, "Shane, it's time to continue your journey. Nik is waiting for you and Alice down by the river."

"He is?" said Shane. "Why didn't he come himself?"

This one started out as a landscape.
Gomez made it into something special. S.B.

"I don't think he was in a big hurry to run into Bento," said Gomez.

"He's afraid of Bento?"

"He respects Bento's territory," said Gomez, reaching behind him to scratch his back. "Who wouldn't?"

"What about the Old Man?"

"He knows you are in the forest, and he knows you are coming to meet him."

"Who told him? Siti?"

"No one told him," said Gomez. "He just knows."

Just then, a low, throaty moan wafted through the trees. It sounded as if it originated not only deep in the forest, but deep within the powerful body of a large animal. Shane cocked his head and listened; he had never heard such a sound. As the moan faded it turned into a *whuuump, whuuump, whuuump* sound.

"The Old Man?" said Shane.

Gomez blinked his eyes slowly and nodded.

"I'll get Alice," said Shane. "Tell Nik to hang tight, we'll be right there."

"Hang tight?" said Gomez. "That's impossible for an orangutan." But Shane, camera in hand, was already running back to camp as fast as his legs would carry him.

A few minutes later, after some hasty good-byes to Anne and Willie and a quick trip across the river in the cable car, Alice and Shane found themselves following Nik along a trail that became less obvious with each step. Then, as if it had never existed, the trail vanished altogether.

"What happened to the path?" asked Alice, tripping over a white root.

"Are we lost?" Shane wanted to know.

"Not lost yet," said Nik. "We are now in a place where man has not walked, a place of no trails."

"Not yet? What do you mean, not yet?" said Shane.

"We're off the map?" asked Alice.

"Looks like it's bushwhacking time," said Shane. "I wish I'd brought a machete."

"Just as well you didn't," said Nik.

"Right," said Shane, remembering Nik's gruesome tale of fast-falling steel.

Nik picked his way through a knot of thick lianas as he plotted a course of least resistance downward over a leafy flank of the ridge. His route led deeper into the twist and tangle of the impenetrable forest. Shane glanced over his shoulder and saw that the foliage had closed seamlessly over where they'd just walked. He hoped they would not become lost, because he knew that no one would ever be able to track them in a forest this thick. He reached into his pocket for his compass and took a quick heading. "Dang!" he said, as he watched the compass needle bounce from one heading to another.

With each difficult step through the forest understory it seemed to Alice that the vegetation became more dense, and the mood of the forest more ominous. Lacy curtains of thick moss hung from the rope-like vines that looped and hung from the branches like streamers. A thick, steamy mist hung in the damp, hot air. The aroma of rot and decay was so overpowering that Alice's nose crinkled with repugnance. Careful not to snag her trouser legs, she edged past a thick clump of rattan, its needle-sharp thorns as lethal as fishhooks at the bottom of a tackle box. In front of her, suspended between two rattan stalks, was a spider's web. In the center was its architect, the yellow and gold spider herself, waiting patiently for the next unsuspecting insect that would glide through the forest only to spend the last moments of its life struggling against the strong sticky web while the hungry spider bore down relentlessly. Alice spread her fingers over the spider's body, and a shiver of dread ran down her spine as she saw that the spider, with its black pushpin eyes and legs as thick as her little finger, was larger, much larger, than her hand.

Then she noticed a nibung palm standing in a small pool of dappled sunlight. The sturdy column of its trunk supported an emerald array of sword-like fronds, which arched from its top like verdant fireworks. She remembered that this was the species of palm Bento had damaged to get at its succulent, nourishing heart.

The air, as they fought their way through the understory, was so thick with sticky humidity that Alice felt she could slice it with a knife, if she had a knife. As they reached the bottom of the ravine the terrain flattened out and the ground beneath their feet, so firm along the ridge, turned suddenly soggy. With each step the soft muck, like the wet mouth of a giant leech, seemed determined to suck the shoes off their feet.

"This is getting to be like a swamp," said Alice, stopping to wipe the sweat from her brow with the back of her hand. She froze in mid-swipe. "Oh geez, there's a leech on my hand!" she whined as she pulled the little wiggler off.

"Yes, but that's all it is," said Nik matter-of-factly. "We're now in a lowland peat swamp. Heaven for us orangutan types."

"Whoa!" Shane said suddenly and a bit too loudly as he pointed to a tree just ahead of them. "Check it out!"

"Shhhhhh," cautioned Nik. "We don't want to disturb them."

Ten feet off the forest floor, clinging to strangler fig roots that wrapped a huge dipterocarp, were two female orangutans. The twisted roots, thick enough to support a suspension bridge, provided the orangutans with plenty of secure hand and footholds. The pair of adolescent red apes were taking turns parting the coarse hair on each other's heads and shoulders with their nimble fingers.

"What are they doing?" whispered Alice.

"They're friends," said Nik. "They're taking turns grooming each other and probably catching up on a little forest gossip. They're looking for parasites and bugs while enjoying the pleasure of each other's company."

"Do you know them?"

"Not yet," said Nik with a sly grin.

"Look at that," said Alice. "They're eating the bugs they find."

"Protein," said Nik. "Got to take it where you find it."

"Hang on a second," said Shane, wiggling out of his backpack, "I want to get a shot of this."

While Shane focused his camera on the pair of females, Alice spotted another orangutan a few yards away. This one was clinging to a slender tree growing beside a decaying giant that had snapped off twenty feet above the forest floor.

"Geez," she said, "they're everywhere, now. What is he doing?"

They watched as the young male inserted a straight twig into a hole in the rotten tree trunk. He poked the hole with the twig a few times, extracted it, and then sucked the glistening dark yellow blob that had formed on the end.

"He's found a hive," explained Nik. "He's after the honey."

"With a stick?" said Shane, focusing his camera now on the honey eater.

"Well, yes," said Nik.

"So he's using a tool," said Alice, looking up at the orangutan, who ignored them. His attention was focused on retrieving as much honey from the cavity as possible.

"Yes," said Nik. "I suppose he is."

"Look at that!" said Alice, her hand shooting toward the canopy that towered over them. Shane and Nik looked up just in time to see a three-foot-long snake wiggle off a branch and glide across a patch of blue sky as if the sky were water. Once airborne, the snake's body took on an airfoil shape, a slender wing that trapped just enough air to prevent it from plummeting to the forest floor.

"That's absolutely amazing," said Alice when the snake had landed on a branch of a neighboring tree in a heap, like a green noodle that someone had flung across a kitchen. "A flying snake."

"Yes," said Nik. "I suppose that is remarkable when you see it for the first time. You know, there are also fish in Borneo that crawl out of the water and into mangroves," said Nik.

"Geez," said Alice. "Evolution happens right before your eyes around here."

When Alice first spotted the flying snake, Shane had put his camera to his eye and attempted to track the flight of the airborne serpent. "Missed it," he

These two females groomed each other for a long time. S.B.

said, looking down at his camera. And then with a whine innate only to teenagers, he said, "Oh man, I can't believe it! I'm almost out of film! I've got like one shot left, maybe two. Dang!"

Just then, another long, breathy call, a sound you could almost see as well as hear, echoed through the forest. Suddenly all the hums, gurgles and chirps of the birds, monkeys and insects fell silent. Even the incessant, nervous rattle of the cicadas ceased, leaving the forest in ominous silence. This time the call seemed to originate from someplace closer—a lot closer.

"He's near," said Nik, nonchalantly scratching an armpit and puckering his elastic lips. Shane and Alice exchanged nervous glances as they followed Nik through a small natural clearing and to the edge of a pool filled with water as dark as India ink. A huge tree with ten-foot-high buttresses stood near the edge of the water. The wedges between the stabilizing buttresses formed pie-slice-shaped rooms that opened onto the forest.

"Might as well sit down and wait," said Nik, stretching out.

"He's coming to us?" asked Alice. "I thought we were going to him?"

"Either way, the result is the same," said Nik. "The Old Man roams the canopy, and he never sleeps in the same nest twice." He pointed to a nest high in the canopy. "That could be one of his nests right up there."

"Why doesn't he sleep in the same nest twice?" asked Shane, sitting next to Nik on the forest floor.

"Orangutans move around a lot looking for food. They're seldom in the same place twice when the sun goes down."

Looking at Shane, Alice said, "I can't believe you're the same kid who was so afraid of the forest just a couple of days ago, Shane."

"Yeah, I've been going through some changes, that's for sure," said Shane, pulling a nearby rattan shoot and biting off the succulent end. "I know it's weird, but I feel totally relaxed here. A couple of days ago I wouldn't even have considered sitting on the ground like this. I mean, who knows what's going to come crawling through here? But somehow, it just doesn't bother me anymore."

Alice scanned the treetops and then looked at her watch, the hands of which still had not budged past their surrender to the midnight hour. "I wonder what's keeping him?"

"He sounds like a busy dude," said Shane, "roaming around the rain forest all day like some sort of canopy cowboy."

"You don't rush the Old Man," said Nik, stifling a yawn. "You know, we walked pass a durian tree a few minutes ago and I couldn't help noticing it was fruiting. If you don't mind, I think I'll just go back and have a little snack."

"Durian? Yuck, that's pretty smelly stuff. On the way over here I had to stay in Singapore," said Shane. "There was a sign taped to the window of the hotel that said, 'No durian eaters.' I guess they were talking about you, huh Nik?"

"Singapore?" said Nik.

"A city, no actually it's a country, an island country. People call it the crossroads of Asia," said Shane.

"Never heard of it," said Nik with a shrug. "Well, I'm off."

"No problem," said Shane as he sprayed his cap with repellant. He stretched out on the grass and pulled the bill of his cap down to shade his eyes. "All this hiking's got me wore out. I might as well take a little siesta while we're waiting."

"Great," said Alice. "I'm going to be the only one here to meet the Old Man when he shows up… if he shows up."

"I think you can handle it, Alice," said Nik with a wink as he climbed into the canopy.

"Shake me if he shows up," Shane said through a wide yawn.

Alice doused her arms and neck with mosquito repellant and leaned against one of the buttresses, feeling a little abandoned. She wondered if they would ever meet the Old Man of the Forest. Maybe he was just a myth, like a centaur or a dragon. Maybe Siti and Yayat had never really seen him. Maybe no one had ever seen him. That's maybe why Nik said no one could find the Old Man unless he wanted to be found. You can't find him? Like, he's controlling whether or not you can see him or something? Yeah, right. That doesn't make much sense, thought Alice.

Alice noticed a daun biru growing in a pool of sunlight beside the inky water. She wondered how such thin stalks could support the plant's huge leaves, which were as big as garbage-can lids. How many leaves were there? Five, six, no seven. How thick and leathery they were in the sunlight, as if they had been cast in bronze. Then, one of the leaves moved. The muggy air was as still as a vacuum, but something had caused the leaf to stir. Then, as if in one of those time-lapse, super slow-motion movies of a mushroom coming out of the ground, an enormous male orangutan emerged from beneath the largest leaf and fixed Alice with a steady gaze.

Alice stared at the orangutan and felt her mind go blank; she didn't have a clue about what she would do next. Out of the corner of her eye she saw Shane napping a few yards away. "Shane" she whispered. When he didn't respond, she whispered louder in a voice that sounded foreign to her, "Shane! Shaaaane!"

"Whasssamatter?" Shane said, pushing his cap back as he sat up.

"I think he's found us," said Alice.

CHAPTER 16

The Valley of Destruction

A lice, who knew it was impolite to point, alerted Shane to the presence of the orangutan with an exaggerated nod of her head. Shane followed her wide-eyed stare to the enormous animal and rose cautiously to his feet. Then inexplicably, perhaps out of nervousness or just plain mindlessness, he turned his baseball cap around backwards. The orangutan looked at them impassively and grunted. His heavy eyelids slid slowly over his root-beer-colored eyes like the cover of a rolltop desk. He remained that way, trance-like, for a long moment. Whoa, thought Shane, the guy's got giant jellybeans for eyes.

"What's that you say?" said the orangutan, opening his eyes at last and scratching his chest with a huge, hook-like hand. It seemed to Alice that the coarse bristles that sprouted from the backs of the orangutan's fingers, hands and cheekpads looked more like cactus thistles, or toothpicks, than hair.

"I didn't say anything," said Shane.

"Something about jellybeans, hmmm?"

"Oh, you know, it was… nothing," stammered Shane.

Remarkably, considering the heft and bulk of the orangutan, and remembering what Anne had told them about how unpredictable and dangerous orangutans could be, neither Shane nor Alice felt themselves particularly knotted with fear. Trepidation, maybe. Caution, certainly. But the initial rush of fear that Alice first felt when she noticed the orangutan hidden among the leaves swirled away like dishwater down a drain. If this particular orangutan, who they assumed must be the famous Old Man of the Forest, meant to harm them, he certainly would have made an aggressive move by now. But this, at least in Alice's estimation, was a peaceful being; it was clear to her that he meant them no harm. And it was also clear to Alice that she and Shane were exactly where they were supposed to be at this moment of their young lives.

"Are you the Old Man of the Forest?" asked Alice, and then thought: Don't be dumb, girl—who else would he be?

"Some call me that," replied the orangutan calmly.

"Do you have another name?" asked Shane.

"Marco," said the orangutan. "Call me Marco."

"Are you a wild orangutan?" asked Alice.

"Wild? No, of course not. I'm a rehab, just like all the other orangutans living in this forest," said Marco, concluding his statement with a pig-like snort.

"You sure look wild," said Shane. "I mean, not wild like out-of-control or anything, but just… you know…."

"Perhaps mature is the word you are looking for," said Marco.

"Exactly, yes, you're right. Mature, that's what I meant," said Shane with relief.

"Have you, uh, lived here long?" asked Alice.

"Let's see," said Marco, rubbing the stubble on his chin, "I was released four years ago next rainy season."

Then the orangutan crabbed toward Alice and Shane, making the dry leaves rustle on the forest floor. With his fists planted firmly on the leaf litter to support his weight, he leaned toward Alice and Shane and began to sniff each of them. When he was finished sampling their adolescent scents, he folded his short hind legs under his body and squatted on his haunches. "Please, make yourselves comfortable," he said.

"We've learned a lot about orangutans lately," said Alice, in an attempt to break the ice.

"Yeah," agreed Shane, sitting cross-legged next to Alice. "And one of the

The lowland forest where we met the Old Man looked a lot like this. S.B.

things we learned is that it's not easy being an orangutan these days."

Marco again closed his eyes and nodded his massive head. "Well, there's an understatement if I've ever heard one. As a species we face a lot of obstacles… most of them placed in our path by humans."

"I know," said Shane, wondering why he felt embarrassed and guilty even though he knew he himself wasn't responsible for the orangutans' plight. "I'm real sorry about how things are for you, but Alice and I, we're not the kind of people who want to harm orangutans, or make their lives miserable."

"We want to help the orangutans," volunteered Alice.

"You do, do you?" said Marco. "And how exactly do you plan to do that?"

"There's a lot we can do," asserted Alice.

"Such as?"

"Well, when we go back home we can tell other kids about orangutans and maybe we can raise some money to help build the Halfway Forest. Ibu Anne said it was needed to help young orangutans learn how to live in the wild," said Alice.

"Or we could raise money to help build a fence that would keep people out of the release forests," added Shane.

"Yeah," said Alice optimistically. "We'll organize!"

"Yes," said Marco. "That would be a start. But these projects you suggest, as noble and well intentioned as they might be, are only temporary measures. They are a start, but they don't address the real issues or get down to the reason orang-utans are so threatened in the first place."

"Well, why do you think you guys are so threatened?" asked Shane, wondering if had missed something.

"The lack of respect your species has for this fragile blue-green ball on which we ride through time," said Marco. "That's number one." He added a kiss-squeak for emphasis.

"Lack of respect?" said Shane.

"Yes," said Alice. "For the environment, that's what you mean, isn't it?"

"I've developed a theory about your species," said Marco, without answering Alice's question. "Are you interested in what the situation looks like from an old orangutan's point of view?"

"Yes," said Alice and Shane simultaneously.

"Can you name another species on this planet who spoils his own home, his own habitat, as humans do?"

Alice and Shane both knew what Marco was getting at, and they agreed with him. It was impossible to name another life form on earth that fouls its own nest to the extent that human beings foul theirs.

"Look around you," said Marco, gesturing with an expansive sweep of his arm, his dark red hair dangling like the fringe of a motorcycle jacket. "This is my world, my home. There are thousands of plants and animals and insects liv-ing here in harmony. You don't see any landfills, do you? No old tires at the bot-tom of the swamp, no aluminum cans, no Styrofoam cups or stubborn plastic garbage bags that time can never rot. No junked cars with their hoods thrown open, yawning among the ferns. There's no dark cloud of pollution hanging over our heads here. You don't see any animals or plants starving while others are well fed. Here in my world we do not poison our water supplies or make war on each other.

Tree by tree, we've losing the tropical rain forests. S.B.

"But in your world..." Marco continued, extending his arm over his head. To Alice and Shane's amazement, the orangutan's arm did not stop when it reached its full length. Instead it kept going as if it was as rubbery and elastic as a Gumby. They watched in awe as it stretched high into the trees. When Marco's clenched fist had reached eighty feet into the canopy above their heads, his thick fingers wrapped tightly around a thick liana, to which he gave a downward tug as if the vine was a rope from which the reality of the forest was suspended. As Marco tugged, the rain forest parted like a leafy green curtain over a theater stage. "Showtime," said the Old Man, a mischievous, toothsome smile curling on his rubbery lips.

With Marco's stage set, the three of them found themselves standing on the crest of a hill, overlooking a valley of mayhem and destruction. In the distance, a fleet of rattling bulldozers spewed billowing black clouds of exhaust into the air. Men with whining chainsaws attacked giant, centuries-old trees. One by one, the trees fell, their fibrous masses cracking and then crashing against the soft earth like giant pickup sticks. They watched as chainsaw surgeons amputated the limbs of the fallen trees and men wrapped thick cables around the logs. Then the logs were dragged by trucks through the yellow ooze and loaded by steel-jawed tractors onto the beds of waiting trucks. The heavy vehicles belched thunderous gray clouds as they groaned against their loads. Slowly they hauled the mutilated corpses of the trees along rutted access roads, bound for mills where they would be sawed into planks and put on boats bound for the western world. Men with red plastic containers doused the remaining slash piles of limbs and stumps with gasoline. Then there were orange flames and billowing, energetic masses of rolling smoke. The flames leaped higher and higher, and the leaves of trees still standing at the edge of the clear-cut curled against the heat. Everywhere, there was the sound of panic as birds and animals tried to escape. But there was no shelter for the animals, and, with the exception of the fallen trees and bulldozers, nowhere for the birds to roost.

Marco released the liana, and the curtain of intact rain forest floated back across the gap, hiding the destructive process that had altered the course of natural history forever.

"There," said Marco as the last of the forest settled into place, "That's a glimpse of how your world looks to me."

Alice and Shane stood speechless and numb.

"Hey!" Shane said finally. "How'd you do that? Was that real?"

"Yes, it's real," said Marco. "What I've shown you extends far beyond any illusion I could ever possibly show you. Tree by tree, acre by acre, it is happening every day, all across the tropics."

"Is that kind of logging even legal?" said Alice. "I mean, isn't that against the law or something? It seems so… I don't know, immoral."

"It's against the laws of nature, but not the laws of man. Man only imagines he has morals, but I could put all the morals man has into my pocket," said Marco.

"Pocket? What pocket?" said Shane.

"Your species thinks their superior intelligence and free will separates them from the rest of the natural world, and that's the greatest illusion of all. They're not separated. Everything that your species does affects the other species. Every day the destruction continues, the boundary of man's world expands and the boundary of mine shrinks."

"This can't go on forever," said Alice. "It's got to stop sometime, before it's too late."

"As long as human beings keep reproducing at their present rate, it's not going to stop," said Marco solemnly. "After the timber is cleared and the slash is burned off, they'll plant rows and rows of oil palms, or rubber trees, or terrace the land for rice paddies. Of course all the nutrients in the soil will be depleted after two or three years, and after that the crops will fail and factories and houses will spring up in their places. Towns and villages will grow together to become part of a big, bustling city. And the rain forest that fell to make room for man's enterprise will be lost to us forever."

Just then they heard a staccato chattering. They looked up to see a large, handsome, black-and-white squirrel, about the size of a Scottish terrier, leaping gracefully from one tree branch to another. It steered its flight with its bushy tail as it made its way through the upper tier of the canopy. They watched as the squirrel joined a troop of leaf monkeys that were feeding on the succulent green leaves of a *Gironneira nervosa* tree. Below, in the middle layer of the canopy, a small plantin squirrel feasted on the winged fruit of a dipterocarp tree, a rare and coveted treat as the dipterocarp bore fruit only every seven years or so.

"See that?" said Marco. "The forest dwellers live cooperatively, each animal occupying its own particular niche. The giant squirrel does not eat the same food as the smaller squirrel. They do not compete for food or shelter, and that's how they can live in the same place. If you were patient enough, sooner or later you'd see another squirrel, a pygmy squirrel that burrows into the forest floor and feeds on bark. He doesn't compete with either of the other squirrels, so he can live here, too. Every living rain forest creature, from the termites, leeches and mosquitoes to the gibbons, orangutans and macaques, lives in harmony with the other species. Of course there are exceptions, and there is some competition among species who are after the same food."

"What do you mean?" said Shane.

"Well, gibbons and hornbills compete with orangutans and macaques for some ripe fruits, but in our own way we cooperate with each other so that we all have access to the same foods. Another form of cooperation exists between plants and animals."

"Oh, I know what you're talking about," said Alice. "The seed thing, right?"

"Yes, the 'seed thing' as you say," said the Old Man. "Plants have to reproduce, too, but they don't have the luxury of moving around the forest as animals do. Once they're rooted, they're not going anywhere. They require help in transporting their seeds from where they are to someplace else."

"So that's what the wind does, right?" asked Shane.

"The wind is a factor with some of the lighter seeds that can become airborne with a good breeze, but wind doesn't help the heavier ones. Many plants produce tasty fruits and delicious nectar that attract birds and insects, and larger animals such as gibbons and orangutans. The animals eat the fruit and then…"

"…they poop out the seed somewhere else," Alice finished for him.

"Right, and the seed, having passed through the digestive tract of whatever animal has eaten it, is softened by digestive enzymes. So a seed that has passed through an animal is deposited on the forest floor with its own bed of fertilizer to help it germinate."

"It's amazing how all this works," said Alice.

"The plants and animals that live in the rain forest are gifts to each other, and that is the beauty of, and the reason for our existence."

"Yeah, you're right," said Alice. The concept of cooperation between plants and animals crystallized in her mind as it never had before.

"But you eat termites," said Shane. "What's that all about? How does that work in the grand scheme of things? I mean, how does your gobbling up those little buggers benefit them?"

"Just like everything else, the termites are here for a reason—for many reasons, actually. Their eating and digestion of fallen trees speeds the degradation process and allows the forest to renew itself more efficiently." Marco craned his short neck and sniffed the aromatic atmosphere. "Can you smell it? The rot of life… ahhh, there's no sweeter fragrance anywhere. Of course in the process, sun bears, orangutans and other animals with exotic tastes eat a few termites. Termites are a very tasty delicacy, as you know."

"Sort of like forest-floor caviar," said Shane.

"They're good sources of protein, too," Alice pointed out.

"True, and protein is as important to an orangutan's diet as it is to yours," said Marco.

"It's amazing the way the animals have evolved," said Shane, looking up at the sunlight filtering through the leafy lacework of branches above him.

"The only species that hasn't really evolved," said Marco bluntly, "is yours."

Alice and Shane looked at the orangutan with puzzled expressions. "What do you mean 'we haven't evolved'?" asked Alice, a little offended. As far as she was concerned, she'd done a lot of evolving just in the last couple of days.

"How could we not evolve?" asked Shane. "I mean, everything evolves and it's pretty well understood that human beings evolved from, well, you know…"

"Apes?"

"Well, yeah, apes."

"Don't flatter yourself, pal" said Marco slyly, pulling a rattan shoot from a young plant and biting off its end. "Besides, what makes you so sure humans evolved from apes?"

"You don't think so?" asked Alice.

"If humans are descendants of apes, don't you think you'd look a whole lot more like me than you do? Why don't you resemble chimpanzees, or gorillas, or bonobos—if you've really evolved from apes?"

"What are you saying?" asked Alice. "If we didn't evolve from the apes, then what did we evolve from?"

"Last year I wrote a term paper on the evolution of human beings," Shane chimed in, eager to impress Marco and Alice with his knowledge of evolutionary science, such as it was. "Human evolution can be traced back to Advanced *Australopithecus*," he continued, stumbling on his mouthful of words but sounding more like a college professor than a high school student, nonetheless. "These *Australopithecus* guys showed up about eight million to two million years ago. And maybe one and a half million years ago, *Australopithecus* became *Homo Erectus*. Around 200,000 years ago, the Neanderthals appeared, but they apparently died out. After that came *Homo sapiens* in the form of the Cro-Magnons. The rest, as they say, is history."

"Yes, Shane, very good, you've studied well, but I don't know how much truth there is to all that. Let's consider some other factors in man's history, shall we? Don't you think it's somewhat remarkable that in all that time—what, almost eight million years—the stone-chipped tools used by both the *Australopithecus* and the Neanderthals were virtually identical?" asked Marco.

"Well," countered Shane, "evolution is a slow process."

"True," agreed Marco. "But what I find puzzling about your theory, strange, even, is that if you try to figure out where, exactly, *Homo sapiens* fits in the evolutionary process, why was there so little progress? What happened to cause Cro-Magnon man to suddenly appear out of nowhere only 35,000 years ago, just about the same time the Neanderthals vanished? What happened to the Neanderthals?"

"War maybe?" Alice guessed.

"Or maybe it was just like here in the rain forest," said Shane. "Two separate species that competed for the same resources and couldn't occupy the same niche. The Neanderthals lost out to the Cro-Magnons. Sort of like a prehistoric Super Bowl."

Marco massaged the back of his neck, and in the dappled light he looked like an aging scholar. "Well I don't know about Super Bowls, but what's really curious about all this is that the Cro-Magnon just... showed up. I mean, they look so much like the both of you that you could pierce their ears, give them a couple of tattoos, dye their hair purple, enroll them in any big city high school, and no one would even notice."

"Hmmm," said Shane. "Yeah, well, it is a little weird if you think about it."

"Right, it is, as you say, weird, but what's even weirder is that when the Cro-Magnons came onto the evolutionary scene, they had tools. These guys weren't getting by with stones chipped into useful shapes, no way. They made specialized tools from bone and wood. And, they had weapons, which gave them a distinct advantage over every other living thing on earth, because with weapons they could dominate. They built shelters with rocks and animal skins, and that gave them mobility. They weren't stuck in their caves for a lifetime. They followed the herds, and the seasons. These guys were not apes, nor did they descend from apes."

"How do you know all this stuff, Marco?" asked Shane.

"How do you two *not* know it?" said Marco.

"I don't know, I guess we haven't read the right books."

"Exactly," said Marco.

"We know a lot about primitive cultures from the art they left behind," said Alice. "You know, cave paintings."

"Yes," said Marco. "And those cave paintings give us insights into their society and culture. For example, we know the Cro-Magnons lived in clans and there was a chief who was in charge. They wore clothing made from animal skins. They had feelings, and they had religion."

"Religion?" said Alice. "Really?"

"Let's put it this way, they had a spiritual consciousness, and that is the cornerstone of all religion. From the paintings that adorned the Cro-Magnon caves, we know they worshiped some sort of mother goddess, and she was sometimes represented by the moon's crescent. And they buried their dead."

"Wow," said Shane. "No kidding?"

"Who knows for sure what that means, but it could mean they believed in an afterlife," said Marco.

"Dang," said Shane. "Talking to you makes me want to go back and rewrite my paper. Seems like I might've left a few things out."

"But, if what you are telling us about the Cro-Magnons is true, how did they learn all this stuff so, you know, quickly?" asked Alice.

"Ah, yes," said Marco. "That's one of the great mysteries of the ages. But an even greater mystery is that in many ways Cro-Magnon man seems connected to an even earlier version of *Homo sapiens* who roamed western Asia and North Africa 250,000 years before Cro-Magnon. So the first *Homo sapiens* might have appeared 700,000 years after *Homo erectus* and 200,000 years before Neanderthal Man," said Marco.

"Now I don't know if it all makes sense," said Shane. "I'll have to do the math."

"You're right," said Marco. "If you're going to limit yourself in thinking about the development of *Homo sapiens* to what you think must be true or you already have evidence for, all you're going to get is frustrated. That's why you have to open your mind to all sorts of possibilities if you are to find the key, or the keys, that unlock the mysteries of the universe."

"Well, how did that happen, anyway?" said Alice. "How did *Homo sapiens* suddenly appear, then disappear, then appear again right in the middle of all this slowpoke evolution?"

"Yeah," quipped Shane. "What are they, aliens or something?"

The old orangutan pursed his lips in what could only be construed as an all-knowing smile, a little like the one associated with Buddha. And then he chuckled to himself. "You humans are funny," he said. "You spend so much time searching the skies for the aliens you are so sure exist. It doesn't even occur to you that the aliens are you."

Out of the Tree

"**H**uh?" said Shane."

"Are you trying to tell us that we are aliens?" asked Alice, a who-are-you-trying-to-kid smirk on her face.

Now it was the Old Man's turn to shrug. "I don't know if you are or not," he said. "Not even an orangutan has all the answers. But I do know that the behavior of human beings, for whatever reason, sets them apart from any other life form on earth. Looking at human beings in relationship to other species on this planet, one conclusion I reach is that your species isn't from here. And if you're not from here, you don't belong here."

"We don't belong here?" said Shane. "If we don't belong here, then where do we belong?"

"I don't know," said Marco, scratching his armpit. "But not here, that's for sure. Your collective behavior has proved that much."

"Well," said Alice. "We've sure seen a lot that we're not proud of, and you've shown us more just now. But people are here, on this planet. Our whole human civilization can't just pick up and go someplace else."

"That's right," said Marco. "Here you are. And I think we need to do something about this 'civilization' of yours."

"Why do you say 'civilization' like that?" asked Shane.

"Well, let's look at some of the people, some of the tribes, that live here on Borneo. Or Papua New Guinea for that matter. Or the Amazon rain forest."

"Okay," said Alice. "We studied the Amazon Indians last year in social studies. They are a very primitive culture."

"What do you think is the reason for the Amazon tribes' being so 'primitive'?"

"The reason?" said Shane. "Maybe it's because they're so isolated."

"Yes, they're isolated. But from what?"

"From us," said Alice. "From civilization."

"Why haven't the indigenous people of the earth, who have been fortunate enough to live unmolested in remote and inaccessible pockets here and there, developed parallel civilizations to yours?" wondered Marco. "They share the same requirements for life that you do. Where's their science? Where's their technology?"

"Where's their GameBoys?" said Shane.

"Where's their cell phones and VCRs and HDTV?" added Alice. "Where are their cars?"

"Exactly," said Marco with a nod.

"Yeah," said Shane. "Why don't they have the same stuff we do?"

"Yeah," said Alice. "Where's their *stuff?*"

"These so-called primitive cultures are about where they should be if they've followed the natural pace of evolution," said Marco. "But maybe we're not asking the right question."

"Well, what is the right question?" said Alice.

"Asking the right question requires thinking out of the tree," said Marco.

"Well, here's one thing," said Alice, after a pause. "How much stuff do people need? At home, the new houses being built are bigger and bigger, and so are the cars, and everyone's always getting more stuff. And you know, they actually complain about having too much stuff. It doesn't really seem to make them all that happy."

"Yeah, I've noticed that too," said Shane. "Also, people seem to spend half their time in their cars, complaining about how hard it is to get around."

"And think what their cars are doing to the air," observed Marco. "You're not the only ones who have to breathe it."

"This is making me think about the Native Americans," said Alice. "I guess they're considered primitive, right? More primitive than us anyway. But they seemed to have things figured out pretty well. They were pretty good at living with other species, with the buffalo for instance. Until white people came and killed off most of the buffalo."

"They killed off most of the Native Americans, too," said Shane.

"So who's more primitive?" asked Marco rhetorically.

"Well, right," said Alice. "But you know, people aren't going to want to become what we call primitive again. And people whose lives are hard now, when they find out about modern things that make life easier, they're going to want those things too. And who are we to say they can't have what we have?"

"So how can we keep all the people satisfied, and not kill off the other species' habitats?" asked Shane.

"Other species' habitats?" asked Marco. "What's your habitat?"

"Good point," said Shane.

"So how can we make human life not destroy other life?" said Alice. "I actually kind of think people might be happier themselves if they figured out how."

"You'll have to use that part of your brain called the imagination to figure that out," said Marco. "Your imagination will help you ask the right questions, and science, in time, will provide you with the correct answers."

"Dang, I feel like I should write that down," said Shane.

"Maybe you should," said Marco.

"This is all so complicated," said Alice, whose mind was suddenly reeling with contradictions and possibilities.

"Life is complicated," said Marco. "At least it is if you're a human being. But I suppose that's what makes it so interesting."

"Do you ever wish you were like us, Marco?" asked Shane.

"That would be impossible. Evolution moves forward, not backward," said Marco, and Alice thought she saw the Old Man wink. "Besides, why would I want to be like you? It's you who should want to be more like me."

Marco kiss-squeaked and reached for a vine that dangled just above the forest floor. He gave it a tug to test its strength, then began his ascent. The sturdy vine supported his weight until he reached a tree limb onto which he pulled his considerable bulk. Alice and Shane watched as Marco, without a backward glance, climbed through the canopy.

"Hey, Marco," yelled Shane. "Where are you going?"

"Going?" called Marco, hanging from a distant limb by one arm. "Weren't you watching? I'm already gone."

"Marco!" yelled Alice. "Come back!"

But the Old Man had vanished.

CHAPTER 18

The Long Call

"Oh, man," said Shane. "Now what are we going to do? How're we going to get out of here?"

"I don't know," said Alice, turning slowly around. Every direction she looked, she saw an impenetrable green wall. Suddenly she was aware again of how easy it was to lose your way in the rain forest. "How could Marco just go off and leave us here?"

"Where's Nik? He said he would come back. Where is he?" said Shane, his voice rising an octave or two. "Nik! Nik!" he called, but the only response was his own futile echo ricocheting through the trees. Unseen behind the emerald curtain, a hornbill laughed.

"Shane, I'm... I'm scared. I wasn't scared when Marco was here, but now I'm really scared," said Alice. "What are we going to do? We don't know where we are, and neither does anyone else. Oh, why did I ever follow Siti?"

"Don't worry, I'll think of something," said Shane, though his mind felt as empty as a new refrigerator on the showroom floor. He scanned the canopy for the liana Marco had tugged to reveal the clear cut. "Where's that vine Marco pulled? If we could only get beyond these trees, maybe we could hitch a ride with one of the logging trucks."

"There aren't any logging trucks, Shane. That was only a trick Marco played for us. It wasn't real."

"Are you sure?" said Shane. "It sure seemed real."

"No," said Alice. "I mean, yes. Oh, I don't know what's real and what's not anymore." Alice looked around at the tall trees, at all the elements that made up the forest, and then said, "Marco is right, we don't belong here."

A yellow spider with a bulbous body the size of a silver dollar dropped down from the canopy on a thin silk thread. It dangled at Alice's eye level for a moment and then retreated back to the canopy on its invisible lifeline. That was when they heard it—a low moan drifting through the canopy. The sound seemed to wrap around the trees like a vaporous boa constrictor, groaning from one direction, then another, as if some phantom prankster was playing with the balance knob on a stereo.

"Hear that?" said Shane.

"It's Marco. Maybe he's coming back for us."

Though there was no wind and the forest was as still as a postcard, the leaves overhead started to shake. Alice and Shane looked up and saw a tight knot of branches and leafy limbs trembling high in the canopy.

"What the heck…" said Shane.

"It's an orangutan nest," said Alice.

"But whose?"

"How should I know?"

The nest stopped shaking and, like the spider, started a slow descent. A few minutes later Alice and Shane peered into the empty nest before them on the forest floor.

"Nobody home," observed Shane.

"Spooky how it just… floated down like that," said Alice. "What do you think is going on?"

"I've got no clue."

"You're always saying that."

"Well, I don't."

"Maybe we're supposed to get in," said Alice finally.

"Get in? Why?"

"I'm not sure, I just have a feeling that this is our ticket out of here," said Alice, stepping tentatively into the nest. "You coming?"

"Well, I sure as heck ain't staying here all by my lonesome," said Shane as he took Alice's hand and climbed into the nest. "Pretty roomy."

"Maybe it was the Old Man's at one time."

The nest creaked, then began to rock to and fro very slowly.

"Sit still, Shane. You're going to knock us over."

The nest ceased to rest on the forest floor.

"Get ready!" whispered Alice, taking Shane's hand.

"For what?"

"I think we're going for a ride," said Alice as the nest levitated above the forest floor.

"Oh man, I didn't sign up for this," said Shane worriedly, peering over the edge of the nest. Defying gravity and supported by nothing at all, they floated upward through the canopy as if they were passengers in a basket suspended beneath a hot air balloon—except there wasn't any balloon and there were no strings. They bobbed past a troop of leaf monkeys, who stopped their frenzied feeding long enough to gaze at them curiously. The troop's alpha male charged along a branch and scolded them angrily. A little farther into the canopy, a colony of upside-down fruit bats blinked at them as they floated past.

"Hey!" said Alice. "I think that was Stellaluna!"

"This feels kind of like an outside elevator I was in once," said Shane. Nearby a hornbill looked up from his muddy task of sealing his mate into a tree cavity long enough to cackle at them.

The lighter-than-air nest finally broke free of the tops of the trees like the sun rising on a new day and skimmed along just above the forest.

"Look! There's Nik," said Shane, pointing to the lone orangutan hanging by his feet in a durian tree, completely at ease in his upside-down world.

"Good-bye, Nik!" called Alice.

Nik glanced up at them with no more interest than he would give a jet flying over Borneo at thirty-five thousand feet.

"He waved at us," said Alice. "Did you see?"

"Naw, he was only reaching for another durian. Look! There's Camp Djamaludin!" said Shane as they drifted over the forest outpost.

"Good-bye, Anne and Iyan. 'Bye, Willie," said Alice as she waved at the three figures seated at the picnic table on the deck, seemingly engaged in conversation. Alice thought Willie might have waved at them, but she wasn't sure. Willie often gestured with his arms when he talked.

Then they felt their nest scrape the tops of the trees and they saw Siti grooming Yayat as they sat peacefully on a branch. "Siti! Siti!" yelled Alice, and the gibbons turned their furry faces toward them.

"Good-bye, Alice" called Siti. "Don't forget us!"

"I could never forget you, Siti," answered Alice.

Unlike the dank air on the forest floor, the atmosphere above the trees was cool against their skin as they sailed higher again. "Look, there's the clear cut," said Shane. "See, it wasn't an illusion."

From their lofty vantage point they were shocked to see a logging scene like the one Marco had showed them. It surrounded the forest on all sides, they now saw. Their entire adventure had taken place on nothing more than an isolated island of trees.

"There's the city," said Alice seeing a dingy brown haze hanging above the indistinct silhouettes of low-rise buildings in the dusky distance.

"There's my village. We're headed right for it," said Shane. "Look, there's the school, and there's a volleyball game going on. I wonder if it's the same game."

"It couldn't be," said Alice. "Could it?"

A downdraft now carried them over the same *gang* through which Alice had followed Siti at the beginning of her adventure. They could see how the maze-like *gang* twisted and turned through the city.

"I see the guesthouse up ahead," said Alice. "There's the culvert I crawled through when I decided to follow Siti."

The nest hovered over the guesthouse's back yard like a spider in its web. Then it floated downward and settled softly on the ground, near the fig tree where Alice had buried Siti's baby.

Alice lifted one leg over the side of the nest and climbed out. As Shane climbed out, his shoelace snagged a branch, causing a limb to spring free. This precipitated an unraveling of the entire nest: another limb popped loose and then another so that in a matter of moments, the branches of which the nest had been constructed lay scattered on the ground.

"Dang!" said Shane. "Glad that didn't happen when we were flying."

"Me, too," said Alice.

Just then they heard the squeak of the rusty front gate and a moment later Alice's dad, carrying his bag over his shoulder, appeared from around the corner of the guesthouse.

"Hi Al," he said when he saw his daughter. "I thought I heard voices back here."

"Dad!" said Alice, her heart pounding in her chest. And then she said, "Uh, where have you been?"

Alice's dad gave her a quizzical look. "At my meeting, you know that. It lasted longer than I thought it would."

"Oh, right," said Alice. "How did it go?"

"Well, it went okay," answered her father. "The Director of the Forestry Research Institute for East Kalimantan was very interested in my book project. He'd even like to see the book published here in Indonesia. He thinks it will be good for the children of Indonesia to learn about the plight of the orangutans. They're the ones who are ultimately going to have to care about the welfare of orangutans if the species is going to be saved from extinction."

"Yeah, that's right," said Alice. "There's only so much an outsider can do. Kids in the U.S. can help raise money to help the orangutans, but it's the kids in Indonesia who will have to do the work."

"That's right, Al," said her father, looking a little surprised at his daughter's sudden grasp of the problem. "But the good news is that it looks as if I might get access to the orangutan's protected forest."

"Cool!" said Alice. "When?"

"Well, not right away, not on this trip. The fires and drought have had a devastating effect on the forest. I might have to make another trip here in a couple of months."

"But, I won't be able to come with you... I'll be in school."

"Yes, I know, but that's just the way it goes sometimes in Indonesia." Then he said, "Aren't you going to introduce me to your friend?"

"Oh, sorry. This is Shane, he's a foreign exchange student from California."

Shane stepped forward and shook Alice's dad's hand.

"An exchange student, eh? Glad to meet you Shane," said Alice's dad. "Anything exciting happen while I was gone?"

"Oh, not really," said Alice sheepishly. "We've just been, you know, hanging out—talking and stuff."

"You guys hungry?" asked Alice's dad. "There's a great little restaurant just down the block. It'll be our farewell dinner. We've got a plane to catch in the morning."

"We're leaving?" said Alice, stunned. "Already?"

"I'm afraid so," said her father. "You sound awfully disappointed for someone who didn't even want to come to Borneo in the first place."

"Yeah, I know," said Alice sadly. "I guess I'm getting to like it here. Hey, can Shane come with us to the airport? He's staying in a village not far from here."

"Sure, if he wants to, why not?" said Alice's dad.

"Do you want to, Shane?" said Alice.

"Yeah, I'd like that," said Shane.

"Great," said Alice's dad. "We'll swing by in a cab and pick you up."

"My host father is a cab driver. If you want, I can ask him if he'll drive us," said Shane. "I know he could use the money."

"Sounds like a plan," said Alice's dad. "Think you could arrange to have us picked up at nine o'clock? Our plane leaves at eleven, and I want to give ourselves plenty of time. In Indonesia you've got to expect the unexpected."

"No problem," said Shane.

The Last
Taxi Ride

A s fate would have it, the unexpected event that Alice's dad was afraid might occur, began as soon as Shane arrived home from his ojek ride and asked his host father, Muloko, if he could drive Alice and her father to the airport the following morning. Bare-chested and wrapped in his sarong, Muloko paced the wooden floor in the small living room and explained that he had another fare in the morning and would not be available. But not to worry, said Muloko; his nephew, Wawan, who was not much older than Shane, had just gotten his taxi permit and would be happy to take them to the airport. What time did Shane want to pick up Alice and her father at the guest house? Nine o'clock? No problem.

At quarter past nine the next morning Alice and her father stood, with their luggage at their feet, under the eaves of the guesthouse. Rain was coming down in sheets so thick it was like looking at the world through waxed paper. A flash of lightning, as brilliant as burning magnesium, crackled through a sky marbled with rolling dark clouds. *Bam!* A loud clap of thunder rattled the windows. A howling wind tore through the palms along the deserted street, and coconuts bounced on the pavement like rock-hard footballs.

"What time is it, Al?" asked her father worriedly, checking his own watch.

"Right now?" said Alice with a mischievous grin.

"Of course right now," said her father.

Alice checked her watch out of habit and was surprised to see the second hand ticking along the perimeter of the face. It had started working again. "Nine fifteen."

"The rain's probably held them up," said Alice's father just as a small, doorless Suzuki van, a species of vehicle as indigenous to Southeast Asia as the orangutan is to Borneo, squealed around the corner and coughed to a halt at the curb.

Soaking wet, Shane hopped out of the passenger side of the van and ran toward the guest cottage. "Sorry we're late. Drivers don't like to drive when it rains this hard. The roads are just too slick. They just pull over to the side of the road and wait until it lets up."

"Well, safety first is always a good idea," said Alice's dad as he and Alice wheeled their suitcases to the curb. "We're okay timewise. This is why I build a little extra into the schedule."

"My Indonesian dad couldn't make it, so his nephew Wawan is driving us," explained Shane.

"You sure this car will make it?" said Alice's dad, eyeing the cab dubiously.

"It's a little funky, but it'll get us there."

"Sounds like it could use a new muffler," said Alice.

"Yeah, that and a few other things, like doors," said Shane, picking up Alice's suitcase and putting it in the back.

"I'll ride in front," said Alice's dad as he hopped in. "You kids ride in back."

Moments later the tiny, tinny vehicle turned onto the rain-slicked main highway and rolled toward town.

"What happened to the dashboard?" said Alice's father, who had an unobstructed view of the windshield wiper motor and the wiring harness that supplied its power. He could not help but notice that the speedometer was stuck on eighty and the tachometer needle was likewise frozen in redline territory. The housings of both the speedometer and tachometer were mounted at odd angles and seemed to have come from a different vehicle. A tape player was mounted on brackets just below where the dashboard should have been and two speakers, no bigger than U.S. quarters, stared down from the roof on either side of the cab. He turned to the back seat where Alice and Shane sat and said, "Do you know enough Indonesian to tell Wawan we're not in any hurry?"

Shane leaned over the front seat and, in English, said, "Not hurry, okay?"

"Hurry? Yes, I hurry," said Wawan. He depressed the accelerator and the little van's treadless tires spun on the slick asphalt, causing the vehicle to fishtail. The intense vibration reverberating in the cab made conversation impossible without the passengers' yelling at the tops of their lungs.

Uncomfortable with the speed of the taxi, Alice's father tapped the driver and signaled with a down-turned palm, hoping Wawan would get the idea to slow down. It was then that he noticed the tattoos on Wawan's arm. Some sort of message was tattooed there in large block letters, of a size you would find on a bumper sticker. Alice's dad wondered what was so important to Wawan that he felt compelled to tattoo it on his arm in two-inch letters. He decided not to ask so complicated a question for fear of distracting Wawan from his driving, but this did not stop him from imagining what the conversation might be like. (What does your arm say? What? Your arm, what does it say? What, Mister? Right there, your arm, what does, look out for that pig!) Wawan smiled at Alice's dad and slipped a tape into the tape deck. The vibrating little wagon was immediately filled with an odd rendition of "Auld Lange Syne," delivered through the miniature speakers at distortion-warp volume.

As the rain subsided, a motor scooter passed the taxi like a mosquito on its way to a blood bank. Some of the scooter riders that sped past wore helmets, but most threw caution, and their skulls, to the wind. If there was a helmet law in Indonesia, it was neither respected nor enforced.

"Wow, look at that," yelled Alice's dad as they whizzed past a family of four aboard a single motor scooter. A young boy sat in his father's lap, hands on the steering bar, while an infant, wrapped in a blanket, rode sandwiched between its driver-father and passenger-mother. "That's something you never see in the States."

"You see it all the time here," said Shane.

A few miles down the road, a few miles outside of the city, was a gash in the earth. Bulldozers had cut a wide swath through the rolling countryside.

"Look," said Alice's dad. "They're putting in a road."

Alice and Shane looked out the window at the red earth, dark beneath the leaden sky.

"Looks like they're putting in a freeway," said Shane.

"It'll be the beginning of the end for the wilderness," said Alice's dad. "That road will open up all kinds of places that should really be left alone, and you know what that means."

"More logging," said Shane.

"More people," said Alice.

"And less habitat for Borneo's wildlife," said her father.

Wawan jerked the steering wheel to the right to pass a motorcycle carrying a single rider. At that exact moment, the four-wheel drive vehicle following them pulled out to pass their taxi and the scooter at the same time, its wheels spinning on the narrow, muddy shoulder of the road. Three abreast, the motorcycle, taxi and the four-wheel drive vehicle sped down the potholed road. The taxi passed the motorcycle; the four-wheel drive passed them both, then shoehorned into the space between the taxi and a bright orange bus whose brake lights at that moment flashed bright red. The four-wheel drive braked, the taxi braked, and the motorcycle rider braked hard, immediately losing the one thing motorcycle riders never want to lose: traction. The rider, a helmetless man in ragged shorts, was fresh out of luck. He held on to the handgrips for dear life while his motorcycle slid out from under him, spinning along the wet pavement on its foot pegs, sparks flying. The rider released his grip and rolled into a ditch at the side of the road as his motorcycle continued its spin out of control. Wawan stomped on the brakes and just as it seemed certain the taxi would rear-end the vehicle ahead of him, he swerved into the lane of oncoming traffic, where a flatbed truck stacked with crates of madly clucking chickens was quickly closing the gap between itself and the taxi. Everyone braced for the inevitable head-on crash. At the last possible moment, the oncoming truck swerved to the shoulder, missing the taxi by inches. When the taxi had cleared the orange bus, which had now stopped because the four-wheel drive vehicle that started the chain reaction had nicked its rear bumper, Wawan maneuvered the Suzuki back into its proper lane.

His nerves gone, Alice's dad reached over and turned down the volume on the tape player, which was blaring an Indonesian rendition of "Sealed with a Kiss." He yelled, "Turn this damned thing off!" a request Wawan understood perfectly.

Alice was poking her head out to see if the motorcyclist had survived the accident. "The guy's okay," she said. "He's on his feet and pushing his bike off the road."

"Unbelievable," said her dad.

Shane, who sometimes rode a motorcycle back home, had kept his eyes closed tightly during the entire ordeal.

The taxi rolled into the outskirts of Balikpapan, past greasy, open-air engine repair shops, mobile food stands and lumberyards. Suddenly Wawan pulled to the side of the road without explanation, hopped out of the van and ran into a dark and cavernous pool hall. Shane suggested that Wawan might not be licensed to drive within the Balikpapan city limits; in that case he would have to ask permission, or pay off the taxi bosses, before continuing their journey to the airport. Shane's hunch must have been right, because in the next block Wawan again stopped and this time yelled something to a young man on the sidewalk. The young man hurried to the driver's side of the taxi. Wawan slid in next to Alice in the back seat and the new driver took the wheel.

Gunning the taxi through the crowded streets, the new driver looked over at Alice's dad and said, "Hello, mister." Then the Suzuki was off again on what felt like a chase scene in a movie. There seemed to be some question about the best route to the airport; the taxi cruised the congested streets aimlessly even when Alice pointed to a sign with an airplane and an arrow painted on it. The driver ignored the sign and kept driving in the opposite direction. He pulled into a gas station a few minutes later to ask directions. Then he made a U-turn onto the main thoroughfare and soon, much to everyone's relief, the thatched roof of the airport terminal came into view.

Alice's dad's forehead glistened with sweat. His shirt, fresh an hour ago, was soaked through with rain and sweat. He peeled off a few bills and asked Shane which driver he was supposed to pay, Wawan or the substitute.

"Wawan, I guess," said Shane. "I mean, it's his rig, right?"

Minutes later, while Wawan and the substitute driver waited at the curb hoping for a return fare, Alice and Shane stood face to face in the awkward way teenagers do in front of their parents.

"That was a pretty exciting taxi ride," said Shane. "Yep."

"Yeah," said Alice, "and I thought the rain forest was dangerous."

"Shoot, the rain forest is a walk in the park compared to an Indonesian taxi ride."

"Whew," said Alice. "This has been an amazing trip. And to think I didn't even want to come to Borneo."

"Well," said Shane, clearing the frog in his throat. "I'm sure glad you made the trip."

"Seems like I've learned a lot in a very short time."

"Yeah, me, too," said Shane.

Just then a shoeshine boy who could not have been more than nine or ten years old approached them and asked Shane if he wanted a shine.

"A shine?" said Shane, looking at his muddy shoes. "But these are tennis shoes."

"Yes," said the shoeshine boy. "Very dirty. I clean, good as new."

Shane and Alice sat side by side as the shoeshine boy wiped the mud from Shane's shoes and then buffed them with a brush.

"So, what'd you learn, Shane?" said Alice.

"Well, I learned a lot about orangutans, that's for sure. And, man, the news is not good. There must be some way for humans and wildlife to coexist on this planet."

"You know, an idea just kind of popped into my head," said Alice.

"What kind of idea?"

"More of a realization, really."

"Well, what kind of a realization?"

"I realize I have a voice."

"A voice?"

"Yeah, you know, a say in the way things are, and the way things will be in the future. Once you realize you have a voice, you kind of have a responsibility to use it. If we tell other people about what we've learned, and educate them about why they should care about what happens to the orangutans, then maybe we can make a difference in the world, even if we are just teenagers."

"Yeah, teenagers get a bad rap. Most adults think we're all just a bunch of slackers."

"The thing is, if we combine our voices with other voices, then maybe eventually the world will listen to us."

"Yeah, well, I guess it can't hurt to try."

"Knowing what we know, and learning what we've learned, we have a responsibility to try. If we don't speak for the animals, who will?"

Shane paid the shoeshine boy and then said, "Yeah, I see what you mean. I guess we've got some promises to keep."

"The promises we make to ourselves are the most important ones," said Alice solemnly.

Shane nodded. "For sure."

"When we get back to the States we've got to start planning how we're going to let everyone know about the orangutans."

"A plan, that's what we need."

The loudspeaker above their heads crackled, and a voice announced the flight to Singapore.

They stood facing each other, and Alice looked into Shane's eyes. "So... you'll call me when you get back to California?"

"You bet I will," said Shane. "And I'll be e-mailing you before that."

Alice looked at Shane and smiled.

"Geez, I hate good-byes," said Shane, suddenly aware of how clammy his hands felt.

"Me, too," said Alice, who felt butterflies rise in her stomach.

"Dang, Alice," said Shane, staring at his shoes. "I wish you didn't have to go."

"I wish I didn't have to go, either, but I do," said Alice, noticing her father signaling to her by the departure gate. Then Alice threw her arms around Shane's neck and kissed his freckled cheek. "Good-bye, Shane, don't be sad. Who knows, maybe we'll return to Borneo together someday."

"Someday," Shane repeated. "Yeah, I'd like that."

Alice turned and quickly walked toward the boarding gate where her father waited. A few minutes later, she was looking out the airplane window at the city of Balikpapan. As the plane banked, Alice could see the tin roofs of the rehab center far below and she thought of the orangutans that lived there, waiting for the day when they would resume their lives in the forest. Alice sighed deeply, then turned to her father in the seat next to hers and touched his hand. "Dad," she said, "There's something I need to tell you."

Some Words You Might Not Know

CHAPTER 1

Rattan
A plant indigenous to Southeast Asia; a favorite food of orangutans

Balikpapan
A city on the southeast coast of Borneo, Indonesia

East Kalimantan
A province in Indonesian Borneo

Indonesia
A country in Southeast Asia made up of over 17,000 islands

Archipelago
A string of islands, such as the Malay Archipelago

Endangered species
A species of plant or animal that is threatened with extinction

Sumatra
Fourth largest island in the world; a neighbor of Borneo

Habitat
The place where an animal or plant naturally lives and grows. The habitat of orangutans is the lowland forest of Borneo and Sumatra

Prepubescent
Young, immature, juvenile

Gargoyle
A drainpipe or spout in the form of an odd or ugly person or animal

Tributary
A river or stream that flows into a larger river

Ochre
A color ranging from yellow to orange and red

Rehabilitation
With orangutans, the process of restoring to a condition of good health and ability to manage independently in the forest

Extinct
No longer existing

Mandi
Indonesian for bath

Malice
Desire to cause harm or pain to someone or something

Microcosmic
A world in miniature

Gibbon
A lesser ape with long arms and no tail. Gibbons live in trees and are found throughout Southeast Asia

Culvert
A drain or conduit under a road, sidewalk, wall

Muslim
Having to do with Islam, the religion founded by Muhammad

Clavicle
Either of two slender bones that connect the sternum and the scapula; the collarbone

Egret
A bird that hunts in shallow waters, like rice paddies. In Indonesia, egrets often roost in palm trees

Canopy
The middle layer of a forest; the part of the forest found between the understory and the crown

Brachiate
To swing arm over arm from one hold to the next

CHAPTER 2

Gecko
Any of various soft-skinned, insect-eating, tropical and subtropical lizards, with a short stout body, a large head, and suction pads on the feet

Conduit
A pipe or channel for conveying fluids

Bacteria
Typically one-celled microorganisms, which multiply by simple division, and can be seen only with a microscope

Virus
A very tiny particle that can reproduce only when it is inside a living cell. Viruses cause many diseases, such as polio, measles, and the common cold

Imodium
An over-the-counter diarrhea medication

Ojek
Indonesian motor scooter taxi

CHAPTER 3

Dipterocarp
Vernacular Indonesian word for a tree found in the Borneo rain forest

Lichen
A special organism that is made up of a kind of algae and fungus. Lichens grow on tree trunks, rocks or on the ground

Buttress
A triangular/wedge-shaped support grown by some trees in the rain forest to keep them from toppling over

Parasite
A plant or animal that lives on or in another animal or plant, which is called a host. A parasite gets food or shelter from its host. Fleas and tapeworms are parasites on animals. Mistletoe is a parasite on trees.

Sanctuary
A natural area where birds, plants and animals are protected

CHAPTER 4

Ulin
Vernacular Indonesian word for a tree found in the Borneo rain forest

Sindora wallichii
Vernacular Indonesian word for a tree found in the Borneo rain forest

Acrophobia
A pathological fear of heights

Incisors
The four anterior teeth in each jaw, used for cutting

Understory
The layer of forest between the ground and the canopy

Nocturnal
Active at night

Slow lory
A small nocturnal mammal found in Borneo

Tarsier
One of the world's smallest primates, found throughout Southeast Asia

Civet cat
Any of several nocturnal, catlike, flesh-eating animals of Africa, India, Southeast Asia and South China, with spotted yellowish fur

Cicada
Any of a family of large, fly-like insects with transparent wings; the male makes a loud, shrill sound by vibrating a special organ on its undersurface

Diospyros
Vernacular Indonesian word for a tree found in the Borneo rain forest

Legume
A plant whose seeds grow in pods. Peas, beans, lentils, and peanuts are in the legume family

CHAPTER 5

Chimpanzee
A small ape with a dark coat that lives in groups in the forests of central and eastern Africa. Chimpanzees sleep in nests that they build in trees. They are very intelligent

Gorilla
A large, very strong primate that is a kind of ape. Gorillas have big, heavy bodies, short legs, and long arms. They live in Africa and are severely endangered

Arboreal
Living in trees. Orangutans are arboreal

Larva (plural, Larvae)
The newly hatched form of some insects and other animals without backbones. A larva has a soft body that looks like a worm and has no wings. A caterpillar is the larva of a moth or butterfly, and a grub is the larva of a beetle

Paraphrasing
A restatement of a passage giving the meaning in another form, as for clearness

Organism
A living thing. Animals, plants, amebas, and bacteria are all organisms

Leech
A kind of worm that sucks the blood of animals. Leeches are found in ponds, rivers and damp soil

Deet
The active ingredient in many insect repellents

Poacher
A person who hunts or takes wildlife illegally

Durian
Vernacular Indonesian word for a

tree found in the Borneo rain forest

Machete
A heavy, sword-like knife

Black market
The illegal and unlawful buying
and selling of animals and other
goods

Artifact
An object made by human beings,
especially one belonging to an earlier time or culture

Gall bladder
A membranous sac attached to the
liver in which bile is stored and
concentrated

CHAPTER 6

Primates
A group of mammals that includes
humans, apes, and monkeys. All
primates have large brains, eyes
that look forward, and fingers and
thumbs that can grasp things

Proboscis monkey
A monkey found in Borneo. The
male is distinguished by its prominent nose

Bintawa
Vernacular Indonesian word for a
tree found in the Borneo rain forest

Liana
A luxuriantly growing, woody,
tropical vine that roots in the
ground and climbs

Nibung
Vernacular Indonesian word for a
tree found in the Borneo rain forest

Serdang
Vernacular Indonesian word for a
tree found in the Borneo rain forest

Epiphyte
A plant that grows on another
plant but is not a parasite and pro-
duces its own food by photosyn-
thesis. Certain orchids, mosses and
lichens are epiphytes

Vortex
A swirling mass; a whirlpool or
whirlwind

Instinct
A way of acting or behaving that a
person or animal is born with and
does not have to learn. Birds build
nests by instinct

Conservation
The preservation and protection of
natural resources

Conservation biologist
A biologist whose main concern is
conserving the environment

Monitor
A person who warns or keeps watch

Malnourished
Suffering from inadequate or unbalanced nutrition

Drought
A long period of time when there is little or no rain

Tuberculosis (TB)
A disease that is caused by bacteria and usually affects the lungs

Hepatitis
Inflammation of the liver

Taiwan Ten
A group of ten poached baby orangutans that were intercepted at the Taiwan airport and returned to Borneo for rehabilitation

Clouded leopard
A leopard species found in Southeast Asia

CHAPTER 7

Cultural barrier
A difference of opinion between people growing up with different-beliefs and customs

Udder
A sac that hangs from the under-side of certain female animals, especially cows, goats, ewes, and mares. It contains the glands that make milk. Each gland is connected to a nipple where a baby animal can nurse.

Culinary
An adjective used to describe cooking or the kitchen

CHAPTER 8

Decade
Ten years

Ibu
Indonesian word to denote respect for a woman

Saskatchewan
A province in Canada

Gore-tex
A modern fabric that sheds water while allowing the passage of air

Homo sapiens
The species of bipedal primates to which modern human beings belong

Academic
Pertaining to areas of study that are not vocational or applied

Primate psychologist
A psychologist specializing in studying the behavior of primates

Peat
Partially decomposed vegetable matter found in swamps and bogs

Rehabilitant
Orangutans that have successfully completed the rehabilitation process are called "rehabilitant"

Proselytize
To attempt to convert someone to another opinion

CHAPTER 9

Camp Djamaludin
A remote forest outpost in Borneo where researchers and forest technicians live while they monitor and study rehabilitant orangutans

Botany
The study of plant life

Vernacular
Common name of plants and animals expressed in native language

Kerosene
A fuel used widely for cooking in developing countries

Fiction
Written work that tells a story or stories about characters and events that are not real. This book is a work of fiction, but it is based on fact

Environmental fiction
Fiction with an environmental theme

Invertebrate
An animal without a backbone; worms, insects, lobsters and sponges are invertebrates

Background extinction
Extinction that occurs naturally, without the influence of human beings

Flora
The plants or plant life of a given region or period. Dipterocarp trees are part of the flora of Borneo

Fauna
The animals or animal life of a given region or period. Orangutans are part of the fauna of Borneo

Land bridge
A strip of land between islands. Many islands that are close together were once connected by land bridges.

Java
The most populated island in Indonesia

Bali
An Indonesian island

Lombok
An Indonesian island near Bali

Subspecies
Any natural subdivision of a species that exhibits small, but persistent, morphological variations from other subdivisions of the same species living in different geographical regions

Cheek pads
The growths on the sides of a mature male orangutan's face

Plantations
A large estate or farm worked by laborers who live there

Julia Butterfly Hill
A young woman who spent two years living in a redwood tree in Humboldt County, California. Her effort spared the tree she named Luna and brought international attention to threatened redwood forests

Transect
A scientific division of parts of a forest; scientists record which species of plants and animals reside in each transect

Reproductive rate
How many offspring an animal will have during the course of its lifetime

Julia Roberts
An actress who brought attention to the plight of the orangutans

CHAPTER 10

Buddha
Siddhartha Gautama, a religious philosopher and teacher who lived in India 563-483 B.C. and was the founder of Buddhism. The name is a title applied by Buddhists to someone regarded as embodying divine wisdom and virtue

Subadult
A subadult orangutan is ten to fifteen years old

Juvenile
A juvenile orangutan is five to ten years old

Kledang
Vernacular Indonesian word for a tree found in the Borneo rain forest

Cambium
In woody plants, a layer of formative cells between the wood and bark; the cells increase by division and differentiate to form new wood and bark

Fibrous
Containing or composed of fibers

Forage
To search for food or provisions

Bandang
Vernacular Indonesian word for a tree found in the Borneo rain forest

CHAPTER 11

Genus
The major subdivision of a biological family or subfamily, usually consisting of more than one species

Species
A basic category of biological classification composed of related individuals that are able to breed among themselves

Umbut
Vernacular Indonesian word for the succulent heart of a palm; a favorite food of orangutans

Biodiversity
A term used to describe the variety of plants and animals found in a particular location or habitat

Alzheimer's
A disease marked by progressive memory loss and mental deterioration associated with brain damage

AIDS
A disease of the immune system characterized by increased susceptibility to opportunistic infections, certain cancers, etc.

HIV
A retrovirus that invades and inactivates T cells and is a cause of AIDS

Copulate
To engage in sexual intercourse

Genetic evidence
Information gained through study of genetic makeup

Data
Facts, statistics or items of information

Longevity
The length of a life

Hypothesis
A provisional theory or assumption set forth to explain some class of phenomena

Reproductive cycle
The length of time between the birth of one offspring and another. The reproductive cycle of an orangutan is approximately eight years.

Quarantine
Strict isolation imposed to prevent the spread of disease

Logistics
The planning and implementation of details in any operation

Hectare
A unit of land surface measurement equal to 10,000 square meters (2.741 acres)

Acacia
Vernacular Indonesian word for a

tree found in the Borneo rain forest

Subsistence farmers
Farmers who grow only enough food to feed themselves and their immediate families

CHAPTER 12

Mahakam
A river in Borneo

Serpentine
Snake-like in shape or character

Resonant
Deep and full in sound

Dayak
People indigenous to Borneo. The Dayaks are to Borneo what the Native Americans are to the United States

Wattle
Flesh lobes hanging down from the head or neck of certain birds such as turkeys and some species of storks

Vermin
Small animals that are hard to control and are considered objectionable

Betel nuts
The seeds of a palm, chewed as a stimulant in many tropical regions together with slaked lime and betel leaves

Emaciated
Abnormally thin

Excrement
Waste matter, especially feces discharged from the body

Compensate
To make payment, recompense or reimbursement to

Abdomen
The part of the body between the thorax and the pelvis; the belly

CHAPTER 13

Avarice
Insatiable greed for riches

East Timor
An island in Indonesia

Deterrent
Something that deters, or discourages from acting or proceeding

Watershed
A region or area drained by a river or stream

Encroachment
The act of trespassing upon the property, domain or rights of another

Legitimate
In accordance with established rules or standards

Sulawesi
An Indonesian island

Demarcate
To determine or mark off the
boundary of

CHAPTER 14

Pasir Ridge International School
A school in the city of Balikpapan

Paramedic
A person trained to assist a physician or give medical treatment in
the absence of a physician

DNA
Deoxyribonucleic acid: a nucleic
acid molecule that is the main
constituent of the chromosome
and that carries the genes along its
strands

Rembrandt
A Dutch painter who lived in the
years 1606 to 1669

Raze
To level to the ground; to tear
down

CHAPTER 15

Essence
The basic, real, or invariable
nature of a thing; substance

Aperture
An opening, a hole. In this case
the hole in a lens of a camera
through which light passes when
making a photograph

Depth-of-focus
The part of a photograph that is in
focus

Compass
An instrument that determines
direction by using a magnetic needle that points north

Daun biru
Vernacular Indonesian word for a
tree found in the Borneo rain forest

CHAPTER 16

Trepidation
Fearful anxiety

Mayhem
The crime of willingly crippling or
maiming another; wanton destruction

Scottish terrier
A small black dog; a breed that
originated in Scotland

Troop
In this case, an assemblage of
monkeys

Niche
The position of a particular population in an ecological community

Enzymes
Any of various proteins originating in living cells capable of producing certain chemical changes in organic substances by catalytic action, as in digestion

Germinate
To begin or cause to grow, sprout

Crystallize
To form or cause to form into crystals

Bonobo
An endangered chimpanzee-like ape that lives in the tropical forest south of the Zaire River in Africa. Humans and Bonobos share between 99 and 99.6% of their genetic makeup

Homo erectus
An early man who walked upright

Neanderthal
An extinct subspecies of humans that lived in the Stone Age

Cro-Magnons
A prehistoric Caucasoid type of cave-dwelling man who lived on the European continent, distinguished by tallness and erect stature, and the use of stone and bone implements

Clans
A group of people with interests, purposes, etc. in common

Spiritual consciousness
An awareness of the spirit or the soul, as distinguished from the body or material matters

Aliens
Belonging to another country or people, or in this case, a visitor from space

CHAPTER 17

Indigenous
Existing, growing, or produced naturally in a region or country; belonging to as a native

Parallel
Lines extending in the same direction and at the same distance apart at every point, so as never to meet

Technology
The science or study of the practical or industrial arts, applied science, etc.

HDTV
High-definition television

CHAPTER 18

Ricochet
The oblique rebound or skipping
of a bullet, stone, etc. after striking
a surface at an angle

Levitate
To cause to rise and float in the air

Alpha male
The male leader of a group of animals

CHAPTER 19

Sarong
A loose-fitting, skirt-like garment
worn by men and women in
Indonesia and some Pacific islands

Getting Involved

There is a lot of information available on orangutans, both on the Internet and in the printed word. Here are a few Internet web sites to help you get started, but I encourage you to follow the links you'll find on these sites to discover what else is available on orangutans and other endangered species.

Balikpapan Orangutan Society
www.orangutan.com

Deer Creek Publishing
deercreekpublishing.com

Orangutan Sanctuary
www.yorku.ca/arusson

The Jane Goodall Institute
www.janegoodall.org

Orangutan Foundation International
www.orangutan.org

International Union of the Conservation of Nature
www.iucn.org

Geocities
www.geocities.com

RECOMMENDED READING

Orangutans:
Wizards of the Rain Forest
by Anne E. Russon
Key Porter Books
ISBN 1-55263-063-3

Song of the Dodo:
Island Biogeography in an
Age of Extinctions
by David Quammen
Simon & Schuster
ISBN 0-684-82712-3

The Malay Archipelago
by Alfred Russel Wallace
Periplus
ISBN 962-593-645-9

Field Guide to the
Mammals of Borneo
by Junaidi Payne, Charles M. Francis
and Karen Phillips
The Sabah Society
ISBN 967-99947-1-6

The Wildlife of Indonesia
by Kathy MacKinnon
Penerbit PT Gramedia Pustaka
Utama
ISBN 979-511-059-4

Orang-Utans in Borneo
by Gisela Kaplan and Lesley Rogers
University of New England Press
ISBN 1-875821-13-9

Reflections of Eden:
My years with the Orangutans of
Borneo
by Biruté M. F. Galdikas
Back Bay Books/Little Brown
ISBN 0-316-30186-8

Orangutan Odyssey
by Biruté M. F. Galdikas and
Nancy Briggs with photographs by
Karl Ammann
Harry N. Abrams, Inc., Publishers
ISBN 0-8109-3694-1

The 12th Planet
by Zecharia Sitchin
Avon Books
ISBN 0-380-39362-X

Dale Smith at work on "What the Orangutan Told Alice" in a Borneo rain forest.

Dale Smith lives with his daughter Alice and their Scottish terrier Kirby in Nevada City, California. He is the author of "What the Parrot Told Alice," and is now working on the third book in his environmental fiction series, "What the Tortoise Told Alice."

Order form

Purchase orders may be faxed to: **530 478 1759**

Telephone orders: **530 478 1758**

E-mail orders: **deercrk@pacbell.net**

On-line orders: **deercreekpublishing.com** or **Amazon.com**

Postal orders: **P.O. Box 2594, Nevada City, CA 95959**

Please send _____ copies of "What the Orangutan Told Alice" @ $15.95 each to:

Name _____

Address _____

City _____ State _____ Zip _____

Please send _____ copies of "What the Parrot Told Alice" @ $11.95 each to:

Name _____

Address _____

City _____ State _____ Zip _____

Please send _____ 1 copy each of "What the Orangutan Told Alice" and "What the Parrot Told Alice" @ $25.00 for both books (10% savings) to:

Name _____

Address _____

City _____ State _____ Zip _____

Sales tax

Please add 7.25% ($1.16 for orangutan book; 87¢ for parrot book) for books shipped within California.

Shipping

For 1 or 2 books, add $3.00 for shipping. Call for information if ordering more than two books.

Payment

_____ check (made payable to Deer Creek Publishing)

Are you a teacher interested in using these books in the classroom? Please visit our web site (deercreekpublishing.com) to download a free teacher's guide for "What the Orangutan Told Alice" and "What the Parrot Told Alice." Ask about our educational discounts.